"Between Hope and Nowhere" is a fictional tale of suspenseful vigilante justice.

Between *Hope* and Nowhere

Clifton Dee

Order this book online at www.trafford.com
or email orders@trafford.com

Most Trafford titles are also available at major online book retailers.

Printed in Victoria, BC, Canada.

ISBN: 978-1-4269-2204-6 (soft)
ISBN: 978-1-4269-2203-9 (hard)

Library of Congress Control Number: 2009912057

*Our mission is to efficiently provide the world's finest, most comprehensive book publishing
service, enabling every author to experience success. To find out how to publish your
book, your way, and have it available worldwide, visit us online at www.trafford.com*

Trafford rev. 11/19/2009

 www.trafford.com

North America & international
toll-free: 1 888 232 4444 (USA & Canada)
phone: 250 383 6864 ♦ fax: 812 355 4082

Introduction

I come to find my seat that is across the aisle from a guy my age, about 25. He looks just as thrilled as me to be taking a bus from Charleston, SC to New Mexico, yuck. He looks up at me and asks, "So, where are you from?" I laugh on the inside when I realize the actual geographical location. Artesia is south of Roswell between two towns called Loco Hills and Hope. I look at him, smile, and say, "I'm between hope and nowhere."

Dedicated to all those who have suffered the demons of childhood abuse. May your hearts find peace.

In loving memory of
Gilbert Bruce Stark

Contents

Chapter 1

All Aboard

As if it were an invitation into my consciousness the bus driver bellows, "All aboard!" I exhale one last drag off my cigarette, take a deep breath, and start up the steps into the bus. With every step I ponder a different moment in my past, present, and future.

My past was filled with a bible thumping, prone to incest, small town, and deranged type of father. This is one of the reasons for my impending vengeful rage that will soon be unleashed.

My recent present is getting discharged from the Navy. Yeah, that was an absolute trip, me a small town kid from Artesia, NM, making his way to the depths of the ocean onboard a nuclear powered fast attack submarine.

Walking past the people who have found their seats I can't help but take a quick inventory of the type of characters that will be sharing this ride. There is the harmless old couple at the front of the bus. About midway sits a beautiful brunette around 30 with her 5 year old son. Finally I start to reach the rear of the bus when I notice a middle aged balding white man sitting next to a 10 year old girl. She looks like the sadness in her heart could bring angels falling to the earth so broken that the spot where they fell would leave a 6 foot blood pool while exploding feathers make their way back to heaven.

I have seen that look before in my sister's eyes. Hence the hatred I have for the man I will definitely make pay. Dear old dad.

I come to find my seat that is across the aisle from a guy my age, about 25. He looks just as thrilled as me to be taking a bus from Charleston, SC to New Mexico, yuck. He looks up at me and asks, "So, where are you from?" I laugh on the inside when I realize the actual geographical location. Artesia is south of Roswell between two towns called Loco Hills and Hope. I look at him, smile, and say, "I'm between hope and nowhere."

There is another burning hatred for two cranked out idiots that decided to brutally murder my Grandfather for nothing more than the money in his pockets and his guns. They currently reside in a New Mexico prison but vengeance will surely find a way.

My departed Grandfather from my mother's side was one of those easy going, quick to laugh, party type of grandpas. He was spending his retirement years in the Gila Wilderness region of New Mexico. A man with a modest but plentiful retirement decided to spend his last days in a little tow trailer on a big plot of land. I guess it must have been the mix of Indian and pioneer that drove him to wide spaces with few if any people.

I would like to think that the recent visions and dreams I have been experiencing are some sort of spiritual guidance from Grandpa. It started when I was under the ocean in that hell of steel and stench of man. I was asleep when a dream got my blood to pumping. The dream was of a warrior brave on a bare back horse. It was a beautiful white horse as tall and strong as the man who rode him. The brave had war paint in blood red fashioned in a hand print on one side of his face. His long jet black hair had a leather band holding it tightly against his head smartly parted down the middle. There were extensions of leather from the band that were adorned with three black and white feathers.

The brave looked at me with an intensity that would bring out the adrenaline in a corpse. As my heart began to race like the thundering hooves of a thousand horses, the brave held up his beautifully adorned spear and bellowed a war cry that sent the birds fluttering wildly. It tapped into my spine like a jolt from an electrified spirit possessing my body. At that moment I woke to four Sonar Techs trying to hold me down and force a hazing ritual on me that involved mummification by duct tape.

I had heard of these rituals and was well aware of the humiliation and pain. Something of that dream and the brave with his war cry had me well prepared for the occasion. I experienced something supernatural. My strength was that of four men. How perfect, I guess the odds were even at that point. I kicked off the two guys at my feet. The two at my arms found themselves smashing their heads together in a bloody kiss. Luckily it knocked them out and by the time the guys that I kicked off got around to come back at me, I had found my hands around a fire extinguisher that cracked them both across the jaw in one fail swoop.

There was never any report of the incident because to do so would mean incriminating themselves for hazing. There was a lot more respect for the new guy from Artesia after that.

Since that incident there was no doubt in my mind that I finally had me a spirit guide and hopefully my guide would see me through this long bus ride to my old stomping grounds. I am certain that in one way or another, the war painted brave would help me seek my retribution that is so intensely focused on the man who I once called dad and the two pieces of scum who murdered my Grandpa.

Sinking further into my seat I can't help but revert into my consciousness and debate the questions that are still haunting me. The questions like, is it wrong to deal out street justice or where is the line drawn? Is it really an eye for an eye? I feel that if someone is murdered then the penalty should be death. What of the other offenses?

This is my conclusion for repeat perversion. There should be an extermination of those people who seem so possessed by demonic addictions that it leads them to sexually abuse children. In my experience I have seen how the fleshly betrayal of a parent can cast demons down the generations that raise their ugly heads in so many different fashions. Ultimately this type of abuse renders most victims hopeless, full of confusion, and sometimes downright catatonic.

People who sexually abuse children don't quit. Rather than have the cycle repeat itself over and over again, it will be in my duty to rid the world of such offenders in grand fashion. Some people would strongly disagree with this thought process but they are those who would try and rehabilitate the offenders and put them back in the world. They would release these demons to repeatedly destroy all the innocence in the world until only darkness prevails. I must walk a little on the dark side myself in order to shine some light.

Feeling more at ease with my conclusion, I begin to relax. The bus feels like a giant cradle with its rocking motion and gentle hum of the engine. The bus driver announces our departure of South Carolina and that we would soon be entering Savannah, Georgia.

Chapter 2

Damsel in Distress

Walking to the back of the bus, the beautiful brunette had a noticeable limp. I could tell that she was in pain as she made her way to the restroom. She finished her business and made her way back through the aisle. When passing my seat, I asked her if she was ok. She leaned with one arm on the backrest of my seat and said, "Nothing a little time and space won't heal." I smiled and said, "I know the feeling."

She asked if she could set for awhile and talk with me. She said her son was fast asleep and she hadn't had grown up conversation in quite some time. Feeling very flattered at her request I quickly moved over so she could sit down.

Her beauty was so profound that the butterflies in my stomach felt as if they had turned into blood thirsty bats. Dark brown hair made its way flawlessly past her cheeks and found a resting place delicately curled on end just below her breast bone.

Sky blue eyes slightly filled with sadness but mostly strength adorned her countenance. She was not tall but her height was a perfect complement to my own. The attractive red sun dress she wore hung to her curves in all the right places, not to reveal too much but enough that the trained eye would be well aware of the drop dead gorgeous body that lay beneath.

She said her name was Keisha. I replied, "My name is Tristan. So where is it that you call home?" "Home is where the heart is." She said. "Right now this bus is my home because my heart belongs to my son who is asleep up there." "As it should be," I said.

I inquired if I could ask some personal questions. She smiled and asked, "How personal?" Joking I told her that I'm not going to get Freudian on her. She agreed. My first question was how did she hurt her leg? She said that it would take awhile to lead up to her current situation. I told her that I had an infinite amount of time on this bus and that I could listen to her talk for a life time. I hoped that she realized my attempt at flirtation. Her blushing chin tilted smile answered that question.

Keisha told me that she met her departed husband in Charleston. He was a carpenter that was building a house next to hers and they met over morning coffee in the front yard. I could tell that it pained her still to speak of him. She said that he was a good man and they married a few months later. Their son was born 9 months into the marriage. Shortly after Billy was born, her husband started getting pale and weak. The doctors diagnosed him with a rare blood disease and he died in 4 months.

Five years later she met a man by the name of Rick who at first seemed to be Mr. Right. Keisha at that point started to refer to him as Mr. Wrong. She said that one night after her late evening shift at the Pancake House she picked up her son Billy from her friend's apartment and returned home. Mr. Wrong was waiting up in the living room with no lights on. When she opened the door she heard him say, it's about time you whore! She thought what the hell? Mr. Wrong stood up from his chair into the moonlight where she could see his face. He had this wild deranged look on his face. She noticed he had a belt in his hands. Keisha told Billy to run next door and wait for her there. As Mr. Wrong approached her she could smell the alcohol on his breath and feel the tension in the air. He asked her where she had been and she said, at work. He said that he had driven by the Pancake House and that he could see that she was flirting with the customers. She said that if buy flirting he means she was politely taking orders then I guess so. He drew back the belt and landed a swing across her face.

In the middle of telling her story to me she stopped and said, "You don't want to hear this crap." With the chance of sounding like an amorous idiot, I said, "If I'm gonna spend the rest of my life with you; I need to know your story." "Sarcasm becomes you doesn't it?" She replied. We both laughed. I think I laughed more to myself do to the fact that I wasn't being sarcastic at all.

Continuing with the story, Keisha said that she had never felt pain like the sting of Mr. Wrong's belt. Not really the physical pain but the betrayal of someone she let into her home and heart. Then when he recoiled and bowed up half stumbling, he kicked her from the side into her knee. She fell and thought well this son of a bitch is going to kill me. She said, wait. I'll do anything. At that point he staggered back to plop into the recliner when he told her that if she continued to flirt at work he would kill her. Luckily the booze must have caught up to him and he started to pass out.

Keisha told me that at that moment she knew she had a possessive, abusive, stalking and all around evil man on her hands. She limped over to the neighbor's house to find her son on the front porch. Billy asked his mom if she was ok. She told him that she would be as soon as they put several miles behind them.

Concluding her story she said, "So here I am." "Wow," I said. "Sounds like your running from trouble and I'm running to find it." "What do you mean?" she asked. "Let's just say that I have recently taken it upon myself to deal out a little justice," I replied. "Justice for whom?" she asked. "Anyone who needs it I suppose."

She went on to ask me about my story. I told her that while away from home my mother had been writing to me and had revealed further information into the psychological state of my sister June. While June was in rehab for her suicidal addiction to meth it was clearer to her the abuse that was inflicted upon her as a young girl. I was aware that something was not right back in our early teens because of vague reports from my sister's friends and herself. We moved everything out of our house while my dad was away for a few days. Soon thereafter my parents were divorced and it seemed that we all kind of went our separate ways.

Details of just how bad the abuse was for my sister have just made their way into the whole truth. Truth that is so ugly it makes me want to vomit at the thought. I went on to tell Keisha about the brutal murder of my Grandpa. I couldn't believe how I was opening up to a complete stranger but also had the deep feeling that she would not be a stranger for much longer.

Keisha told me that she should get back to her seat and check on her son Billy. I agreed. The bus was on a steady hum and feeling comfortable. I laughed at myself as I often do when feeling exceedingly blessed.

All of the sudden the comfort of my thoughts subsided and my body began to feel hot. The hair on my arms and back of my neck began to stand on end. My heart began to beat like a double bass drum set. My senses seemed to increase tenfold. I could smell the lead on the pencil behind the bus driver's ear. I could smell the sour cream and onion chips that were in the carryon bag the elderly lady had at the front of the bus. Although Keisha was several seats ahead of me, I could smell the vanilla shampoo in her hair. Not only shampoo, but I could distinguish two different vanilla's which I assumed was the difference between the formula for the shampoo and the conditioner. Like a blood hound, I'm sure I could have described any scent on the bus and then some. My ears seemed to be just as sensitive as well as my sight.

Wondering what was going on I soon realized that my spirit guide was racing on his horse parallel to the bus. He had one hand on the reins and the other held his spear up over his head. He let out his bellowing war cry and my heart started beating even faster. Wait a minute; I thought to myself, I'm not asleep.

Can I actual have a guide that would come to me in a completely awake, lucid, and sober state? Then I started to question my own sanity.

I asked the guy across the aisle if he saw something strange outside my window. He replied that he saw nothing. Well I'll be damned, I thought to myself. Insane or not I'm going to accept whatever it is that my vision wants me to accept.

About that time an older model Cadillac began to pass the bus. The caddy was as dark as the look in the driver's eyes. The driver honked and swerved aggressively in front of the bus slamming on his brakes a few times. Keisha looked back at me and exclaimed its Mr. Wrong!

The bus driver calmly said, "What the hell is this guy's problem?" I'm sure as a professional bus driver he had seen it all. I walked up to Keisha's seat and said, "Don't let on that you know this guy. I'll handle this." About that time we seemed to catch a brake and Mr. Wrong turned off onto one of the side roads. I notice that we were getting closer to the city limits of Savannah. Perhaps Mr. Wrong noticed this too and realized that we were getting closer to cops.

I walked up to the first empty seat at the front of the bus to get a feel for what the bus driver was thinking. I asked him when we were going stop and he said there was a station 2 miles ahead and he needed to stop there to transfer passengers. I asked the bus driver, "I wonder what was up with that guy on the road?" The bus driver calmly said, "Who knows? I've seen road rage in all sorts of fashions. No big deal though, I'll bet he's off to bother someone else." After realizing that the bus driver wasn't fazed at all by the incident, I could relax and feel confident that whatever takes place in Savannah probably would not be traced back to me.

Grinning at the thought of being able to deal out some justice, I walked back to check on Keisha and Billy. She asked me what I was smiling about and I simply stated, "I'm blessed." A little confused she asked, "What am I going to do?" I asked her, "What is your destination?" She told me that she had purchased a ticket to take her as far as Abilene, TX and that from there her aunt from Lubbock was going to pick her up.

That was the exact bus route I was going to take but I know that I must handle this Mr. Wrong situation. I told Keisha that I had some business to take care of in Savannah and that I would find my way to her neck of the woods eventually. She stated that she would probably never see me again. She inquired as to what my business in Savannah involved. "Let's just say that your business is now my business and you will never have to worry about Mr. Wrong again."

Her son had woke up and asked me who I was. I held out my hand to shake his. We shook. I looked him in the eyes and said, "One day I hope that we can be best friends." I asked Keisha how I could locate her in Lubbock. She said that her aunt was the owner of a restaurant called Big Beef. "Cool," I said, "I'm sure I can remember that." I told her that for whatever reason she does not hear from me and wondered what I might be up to, that she could call my aunt at her restaurant, Old West Burgers, in Artesia. We laughed at the coincidence.

The bus pulled into the station. It was around dusk and with my senses still very keen I could tell that it would be raining soon even though there wasn't a cloud in the sky. Exiting the bus, the driver said that he was on time and that they would be departing in ten minutes. Holding Billy's hand, Keisha looked at me and said, "Be careful." Feeling the presence of my guide still in my blood, I told her "Don't worry about me; I've been known to have divine intervention."

Keisha gave me a hug and I shook Billy's hand. They walked toward the restrooms and I grabbed my bag from under the bus. Walking past the crowd of people waiting to start their own journeys I realized that my adventure had started to take a very interesting turn.

Chapter 3

Savannah

Accepting my spiritual guidance, I knew that hearing my brave's horse whinny was only a sound for me and that something exciting was about to take place. My eyesight seemed very vivid and at the forefront of my senses.

Looking down the street I saw the front end of a older model Cadillac barely sticking out of an alley that ran perpendicular to the street the station was located. Upon further examination the black Cadillac had the exact same scratch running down the front right corner panel. It was a block down the road but I could make out the reflection of Mr. Wrong in the side window. He was leaning against the wall. He slowly would peer around the corner to look this way. I knew this sick bastard was scoping out the situation.

My advantage was that he didn't know me and that I was so ready to kick some ass that my feet barely touched the ground.

I seemingly floated to the next street running parallel to his. My plan was to back door his location by coming down his alley from the next street. As I quietly made my way about 10 feet from the dumb ass, he was still sneaking peaks around the corner. "Beautiful isn't she?" I said in a tranquil voice. "Who the hell are you?" He asked. "I'm the man about to balance the scales of justice you piece of shit!"

He took a swing at me and I ducked. He threw another fist missing me as I leaned back. "It takes a real big man to beat up on a woman," I said sarcastically. "Screw you," he said." My reply was, "Is that the belt you hit her with in the face?" He dove for me and I stepped to the side. Mr. Wrong fell flat on his face. While he was on the ground I thought it was time to introduce some of his own medicine. I landed one foot solidly on his throat as he lay on his back. Then I made sure the other foot came down on his stomach to knock the breath out of the fool. He no longer seemed to have that dark cocky look in his eyes but more of despair. I could feel his arrogance disappearing as I quickly reached down and removed his belt. I positioned both feet on top of each of his arms as to secure him from any defense and began to swing the belt as hard as I could across his face. After about ten licks, blood started to fly and as Mr. Wrong started crying and blinking through the blood I figured there was only one more dose that needed administered. I thought an eye for an eye as I remembered Keisha limping. I grabbed his right leg and propped his foot on the bumper of his car. "Please don't," he begged. "Too late," I replied as I jumped into the air and landed down on his knee. The cracking of his bones sounded like a head of lettuce being torn apart.

Almost simultaneously Keisha's bus was passing. She was looking out the window and saw me standing over Mr. Wrong with a look of satisfaction on my face. Her eyes followed me as the bus past the alley. I gave her a solemn nod and she blew me a kiss.

I knelt down and said in a somber voice, "If you ever try to find her, if you ever try to hurt anyone else, there will be a justifier to balance the scales. Do you understand?" Mr. Wrong, without saying a word, nodded in agreement. Backing away from him, I said, "Now, I need some wheels since your dumb ass interrupted my journey. I think I will borrow yours, agreed?" He nodded again in agreement. I threw the belt at him and opened the car door. The keys were in it and it had a stereo. Cool, thinking to myself, I can have some traveling music now. I laughed to myself and thought I am so blessed.

Driving out of the ally and into the street, I decided to go toward the bus station and find some place to eat. I turned just past the station and saw a Pancake House. Smiling at the coincidence, I pulled the Caddy into the parking lot. Looking toward the windows at the people inside, I noticed the balding man and little girl from the bus. They were sitting together at a table eating.

Just as I was thinking that I could relax I hear my brave's war cry and hoof stomps of his horse. Man, can justice never take a rest? Apparently my excursions would be plentiful and full of surprises. Now my senses were again peeking, blood pumping, and rage building.

Approaching the diner, I could see that the little girl had excused herself to go to the bathroom. There was apparently someone already using the bathroom because the little girl was patiently waiting outside of it.

I walked in that direction slowly and looked toward a waitress that told me to sit wherever I wanted. I took the booth table closest to the restrooms. The little girl was standing three feet away from my table. I saw the perverse pedophile looking son of a bitch turn around and check on his latest victim. He turned back around and began to eat.

Whispering to her, I got to the point. "Does he hurt you?" I asked. With a solitary tear falling from her broken eyes, she nodded yes. "Would you like to go home?" Again she nodded yes. I told her to go into the bathroom and not to come out until a police officer came in to get her. She seemed to understand the situation and as soon as the bathroom door opened she entered and I could hear her lock the door.

I got up and slowly walked to the table where the sick bastard sat. Standing over him I leaned and said in a voice only he could hear, "If you cherish your life then you won't say a word." I sat down across from him and he said in a quivering voice, "What do you want?" "I want you to get up and accompany me to the ally." Then he said, "My daughter is in the restroom." My reply with teeth clinched and trying to stay calm was, "We both know that if she's your blood or not, the only thing you see her as is a piece of meat. Now get your ass up and let's go outside."

Shaking a little, the child predator got up and walked outside with me following him. Outside I told him to walk toward the ally. Approaching the ally the bastard turned and said in a fearful voice, "You got it all wrong. I don't know what your insinuating but I would never hurt that little girl." "Tell me," I said, "and think real hard before you answer, is she really your daughter?" I had to fish around a little to make absolutely sure that I was making the right justifying decision. Now that he was really getting nervous, I guess he was going to slowly shed a little more truth on the subject. He said, "No, she is not really my daughter." I said, "Who is she?" His answer shocked me as he said that he had bought her through the internet. "You sick son of a bitch!" I exclaimed. I stepped toward him and he said, "Wait, I was never going to hurt her. I was trying to save her." The wind picked up and sure enough, here came the rain I predicted. My senses increased and I could swear that if pedophilia had a scent then this perverse bastard reeked of it.

Baldy got on his knees and started begging. "Please don't hurt me," he said. About the same time he knelt down I noticed a gun handle sunk into his boot then the unexpected happened. I'll be damned if the sorry excuse for a man reached down for the gun and said with a straight face, "She likes it." Totally shocked at his extremely sudden change in demeanor, I soon realized that I had a demon to exercise. I thought to myself, let the games begin.

Before he could grab his gun I kicked his hand and landed a down striking blow with my right fist that knocked him out cold. Thinking to myself, Damn, I need this demon awake for what he has coming. I picked him up and threw him over my shoulder. I sat him down on some steps leading to the rear of the diner. Leaning his upper body against the railing, I took some near buy discarded extension cord and bound his hands behind him. I then secured him to the railing. Buy this time the rain seemed to fall so fast that it was stinging my bare skin. With my heart still racing and my mind going out of control, I had to do some pacing and contemplation. This was the moment of extermination. I was so sure of my decision that the people plagued with this type of perversion should all die. Yes, this was the moment of truth. Can I do it? The sick bastard had been out long enough so I started to slap his face and ask him, "Is anyone in there? Can the demons come out and play?" I pulled a hunting knife from my boot strap and waved it slowly in his face. He said, "You don't have to do this." "Oh, but I do," I said softly. Surprisingly though, my conscience was letting me know that I was no killer. However, I have proven to myself and others that I could deal out justice in an eye for an eye fashion.

As Baldy started to regain more of his faculties, I told him, "It must be your lucky day. I've decided to give you a choice. As payment for destroying that little girl's innocents and for ruining her life for sure, you can give up your eyes or your balls. The sick bastard said, "Go to hell." I replied, "Now why would I want to see your birthplace? So which is it?" He had no reply and I said, "Times up!" At that moment I decided to rid the man of his fleshly tool that has shaped demons and robbed young girls of any chance of living a normal life. My knife sunk hard with a plunging blow to the groin area of the demonic son of a bitch. I stepped back, wiped the blood off my knife using his shirt, and looked over the screaming idiot. He was looking down to what used to be his instrument of degradation and abuse. All I could think of to say at that point was, "Justice is served!"

I quickly walked to the front of the diner and entered it. I asked the waitress if she recalled seeing the little girl sitting with the bald man at that table. She said, "Oh yes, you mean Savannah." Wow, I thought to myself, what another coincidence. I must be on the right track to something. I told the waitress that I thought Savannah was a missing child and that the man was probably up to no good. I told her to call the police, that I saw Savannah go into the restroom, and that I thought the bald man went outside. I explained to the waitress that I had to leave. I hoped that no one would know why I had to make such a speedy departure. I believed that everyone involved would see the situation for what it was, justice.

Walking swiftly to the Caddy the rain was starting to die down a bit. I got into the driver's seat and put on the seatbelt. Just as I was putting the car into reverse I could see that Savannah was peeking out of the bathroom door. I think she could sense that things were going to change for her at that point because she had an air of relief surrounding her. She looked straight through the diner into my eyes and gave me a wave. Once again I returned someone's gesture with a solemn nod and I could read her lips say thank you. I pulled away into the traffic and began my quest once again.

Chapter 4

Montgomery

Leaving the city of Savannah, heading west toward Alabama, I rolled down the windows to my new found Cadillac and smelled the freshness of the rain cleaned air. I was feeling very calm at this point. I had dealt out some much needed balance and felt very comfortable with my new found position as a vigilante. I could live with the fact that I hadn't killed anyone but still had relayed some much needed punishment.

Looking ahead I could see a man about my age thumbing for a ride. Moving closer I could see that it was the guy from the bus who sat across from me. I pulled over just ahead of him and waited for him to approach the vehicle. He came to the driver's side window and leaned in asking if he could catch a ride heading west. I said, "Hop in." He threw his bag into the rear seat to accompany my own and jumped into the passenger seat. The guy asked, "Aren't you the dude from the bus?" "Yep," I said. Then he proceeded to inquire with a puzzled look on his face, "Isn't this the car that was going all crazy on the road?" "Yep," I replied with a grin and chuckle. "So what's the story man?" he asked. "Let's just say that I am blessed and leave it at that," I said with an even bigger smile. "Well all right then. Let's roll," the guy said with enthusiasm.

Rolling on is what we did. What we did even surprisingly better was converse. It was nice to be able to play verbal volley with a worthy opponent. Not that I am well versed, it's just that we seemed to have so much in common. Our sense of humor was on the same level and we were both very quick to laugh. He said that his boisterous laugh was a gift from his Grandfather. I told him that it was the same for me.

Further inquiry led me to his name, Jason. I told him that I was Tristan. Jason was predominantly Anglo Saxon like me however; we both had the lineage of an American Mutt. He was sleeved with some very interesting tattoos. His hair was growing out after a slightly apparent Mohawk cut. His jeans were tattered all the way down to his old school black and white Converse high tops. He was wearing a blue mechanic uniform shirt that said Bob on it. He told me the shirt was a thrift store special. A long chain secured his wallet that stuck out of his back pocket. I could see that the wallet had a design of cannabis on it. I asked him if he smoked. He looked at his wallet then back at me smiling and said, "A little. Do you?" I told him that it had been a very long time and to do so would probably blow my mind. "Nah," he said, "the stuff I have is bunk. It probably wouldn't even faze you." "I better not," I stated, "maybe further down the road." "Suit yourself dude," he said. I asked him why he was thumbing and not riding the bus. He told me that he had just enough money to get to Savannah then his resourcefulness would have to kick in to continue on his pilgrimage. I asked him what kind of pilgrimage. He told me that he was just traveling coast to coast, stopping for short periods to work odd jobs or temp jobs in order to make his way to the next stop wherever that might be. He said that he had already been from California to Vermont and was making his way back to California. Jason stated that in his elderly years he wanted to have something interesting to tell his grandchildren. I told him that if he stuck with me I'm sure we would create some real compelling stories.

I could tell that Jason and I were kindred spirits. I felt very much at ease with him around as if I could trust him with my life. One good sign was that my intense visions were currently at bay. This could surely mean that I had found someone on my journey that was a righteous person and how cool that he was becoming my friend.

It was getting late and I was feeling very tired. I decided to start looking for a motel. There were too many small towns to count and eventually we stumbled across another one that was nothing more than a gas pump and a 5 room motel.

I pulled over, got out of the car, and started to walk up to the motel office. Jason followed. Upon entering the office I could see an elderly man and woman sitting on an old yellow couch. They were holding hands and watching TV. Could it be? I'll be damned. It was the elderly couple from the bus. I looked at Jason and said, "Man if this just doesn't beat all. It's official. I have dealt with in one way or another every person on that bus." About that time an extremely gorgeous blond about 25 with curious grey eyes came walking from behind a privacy wall where she was filing her nails. She blew a bubble with her grape bubble gum and asked, "Can I help yawl?" I told her that we needed a room for the night. She said that we had just made it on time because four rooms were reserved leaving only one available. She grabbed the keys and handed me number Five. I looked at Jason and said, "Excellent, five is my lucky number." He said, "Woe, so is mine dude."

I asked her who the elderly couple was on the couch. She said that they were her grandparents and they actually owned the motel. She runs it for them in the summer while on break from college. "My name is Ivory," she said. I told her our names and asked if her Grandparents just got back from a trip. She said that they had. "They look very much in love. How long have they been married?" I asked. She said that this summer they were celebrating their fiftieth wedding anniversary. They got married back in 1945.

Curiosity got a hold of me and I asked Ivory, "Who would reserve four rooms all the way out here?" She said that her college friends, predominately female, were coming to visit and party a little. With that little bit of information me and Jason started smiling uncontrollably and I think we even did a little dance on our way out of the office and toward our room.

Approaching door number five I said to Jason, "This room better have two beds or your ass is sleeping on the floor." He said jokingly, "Oh come on, you know you like me enough to share a bed with me." Sarcastically I said, "Only if the bed was 30 feet wide and you stayed on your half." He said, "I bet you wouldn't say that to the girl on the bus that you so obviously had the hots for." "Was it that noticeable?" I inquired. "Dude, when you looked at her, it was like watching a wide eyed kid for their first time in Disney Land," he said.

I told Jason that I did in fact have deep feelings for her and that her name was Keisha. I told him how weird I thought it was because I had only met her for that brief encounter. Yet, it felt as if I had known her all my life. Jason told me I must have stumbled on the rare phenomenon of a soul mate. I told him that I would probably lose track of her and have to move on. Jason said that he had heard of strange things when it came to soul mates and that mine and Keisha's paths would probably cross when I least expected it.

Jason said, "Hey bro, I wonder what kind of college chicks are going to show up tonight?" "Beats me," I said. "Besides I'm so tired I'm gonna crash." "Suit yourself dude. I'm gonna stay up a little longer to scope out the scene."

Waking up to music, I look at the clock. It said 1:00 am. I slowly made my way to the curtains and peeked outside. I could see eight pickups. They were parked four in a row backed up to each other so that the four tailgates on one row were facing the tailgates on the other row. Like two long bench seats the tailgates were adorned with smiling, talking, and laughing college age females. I thought where is Jason? Looking a little longer outside the window, I could see him standing by the barrel fire. He was next to, could it be, a keg. Feeling a little rested from my two hour nap, I felt like I could really use a beer and company.

Walking outside into the summer air, I could sense that this was gonna be one of those laid back, mellow, golden type of parties. Someone was playing Reggae music and I could smell the scent of what must have been Jason's bunk stuff. Although he claimed that his stuff was no good, I could see that this crowd of girls had a Rasta eyed, serene, and giddiness about them that was probably the result of partaking of the herb.

Moving further down the party aisle past the barrel fire I reached the keg. There were plastic cups on hand and I grabbed one. While pouring a nice cold one, Jason finally turned around from talking to one of the ladies and said, "Nice of you to join us dude." Then he started to make an announcement, "Ladies this is Tristan." I then heard one of the most beautiful sounds ever, sixteen beautiful college girls saying in unison, "Hi, Tristan." It was enough to make any man blush a little. "Hello Ladies," I replied. Everyone started talking amongst themselves. Jason raised his cup to me in toasting fashion and said, "Party on man." I returned his gesture with, "Party on."

Jason turned back around to continue his flirtatious conversation with his new found friend. I quickly finished my first cup of beer and began to fill another. Ivory, the granddaughter of the owners of this fine facility, came walking over to me. She said, "Slow down cowboy, we've got all night." She was making a very obvious move on me as she leaned with her head on my shoulder and said, "So what is your story, brown eyes?" I told her that right now I had the most beautiful woman at this party making an attempt at me and that I must apologize but my heart is elsewhere at the moment. "Suit yourself Sexy, but if you change your mind, I'll have my eye on you all night." I told her that I would surely keep that in mind. She continued on dancing softly with herself, careful not to spill her beer, and made her way to one of her friends who was watching the whole encounter.

I decided to distance myself from the crowd a little. It is quite interesting to view a party like this from outside the glow of the fire. I thought the view from the top of the roof would be cool. One of the pickups was close enough to the porch roof that I easily made my way from the tailgate, to top of the pickup, and then to the roof. I didn't even spill a drop.

Sitting there I could see everything with a bird's eye view. I must have caught some sort of contact buzz while walking through the clouds of smoke to get my beer. I felt very much at ease and somewhat surreal. The funny thing was that I could make out the shadow of my spirit guide in the distant glow of the fire. He was sitting by his own dream like fire with his horse close by. This made me feel safe and at ease.

Jason eventually made his way to my position and it seemed that we talked for quite some time. We talked about philosophy and music. We talked about family and friends. It seemed as if we covered just about all the things in life that makes it worth living. Jason had a good looking red head looking up at him the entire time we were talking. It was the girl he had been flirting with. He finally looked at me and said, "Dude I got to go be with her." "Don't let me stop you, Tomcat. Go do some prowling," I said. Everyone finally made their way to bed.

The next morning I woke to Jason opening the door to our room. He was as happy and energetic as a little kid in the zoo. He brought in some doughnuts and coffee. "Dude..... Dude......

Dude!" He said with a big ole smile on his face. My reply was, "Have fun last night?" "Did I ever, man!" He said as he laid the doughnuts and coffee on the table. "I'm not one to kiss and tell but you're my bro right?" "Of course," I said. "So are you all in love or what?" Jason's reply was, "Bite your tongue mister! All I'm trying to say is I had the night of my life last night." I agreed that it was one to remember.

Reminding Jason of some of our conversation last night, I asked him if he remembered telling me a little about his dad. He said that the talk was a little cloudy in his mind. Continuing he said, "I didn't get all emotional and talk about the way I used to get my ass beat, did I?" "Yeah, you did," I said, "It sounded like you used to be a punching bag for your old man." He told me, "Just forget it Tristan, it's all in the past." I told him that last night it didn't sound like he was ready to forget it. I told him that he had said his father resided in Montgomery, Alabama. I told him that we were headed directly by there and that we should at least see if the man was around to get a taste of his own medicine. Jason said that he really didn't have the desire to dish out some retribution but that he would like to have a few words with the man. I said, "Great, it sounds like a plan."

Cruising down the highway we were making our way west through Georgia with our destination being Montgomery, Alabama. We had plenty of time to talk. I shared with Jason my past, present, and my vigilante future. I felt as though I could trust him with anything so I gave him the details of what went down in Savannah. After giving him the cold hard facts he looked at me and said, "Damn Cochise, sounds like I'm traveling with a real live renegade!" He asked me if I could at least play it cool when we get to Montgomery. I told him that it all depends on what I'm guided to do. He said, "Let's hope your guide takes a little vacation, OK?" "Can't make any promises," was my reply.

Heading further west with still a lot of time to kill, I told Jason that friendship meant a lot to me and that I was glad to call him my friend. He said, "You're not gonna get all sentimental on me are you?" "I'm just saying, bro." "I know," he replied. Jason got a little excited at that point and said, "You got to hear this song I have on CD." He reached back for his bag and pulled it over into the front seat. Reaching in the bag, he pulled out his portable CD player and CD case. "Now where is it?" He said as he fumbled around. "Ah ha, here it is." He grabbed the CD and pushed it into the car stereo. He told me that this was a new artist by the name of Clifton Dee. He said that he really hadn't listened to it much but that there was one song on the album that reminded him of the time we had last night. It was in the Alternative Rock genre and started out with a guitar riff that was fast and strong but then gave way to the somber sounds of a cello. Most of the song was a fast blur and kind of hard for me to understand but the part that stood out was the mellow chorus that went a little something like this,

One peaceful night my brotherhood brews.
You know the night,
the path to choose.

Right wing or left,
we know the way.
Amid the mind of the eagle,
balance upon us, soaring today.

If bloods on the knife,
then our hands share the stains.
Only future remains,
now you're my brother for life.

I told Jason that I liked that song very much and asked, "What is the name of it?" He told me again that the Lyrics were by a new artist named Clifton Dee and that the name of the song was "Sanction."

Continuing on, Jason told me that the last he had heard about his dad was that he was showing signs of Alzheimer's. Jason's half sister had told him a year ago that they were starting to process the paper work to admit him into a nursing home. It seemed strange to me but when Jason got to this part of the story he seemed to be a little sad. I asked him, "Why on earth would you care even a little about a man who used to kick your ass?" Jason explained that he wasn't quite sure but for some reason he still considered the man his father and that he worried about his condition. I said, "I guess there might be a little room for forgiveness in this world. However the last time I forgave someone, they turned around and screwed me." I told Jason that I must be really jaded. I told him of the scripture where Jesus had stated that if a man hits you on your check then you should offer him the other. I told him that currently the only thing I have to offer the world is both of my middle fingers and held them up in a fashion that surely defied everything. Jason laughed and said, "Your crazy dude."

Nearing the outskirts of Montgomery, Jason told me to make a right turn down some rural dirt road. We came to the drive way of an old farm house that had good structure but needed some paint. The house was one that I had often envisioned as a type I would enjoy owning. It had a porch that surrounded all four sides of the first story. The second story had a balcony that accompanied what must be the master bedroom. Sitting on that balcony was Jason's half sister who was smoking a cigarette. We finally came to a stop at the end of the drive way and was greeted with barks and growls of two Doberman dogs. Jason quickly jumped out and said, "Heel!" The dogs surrendered to his command as they sat down. Jason petting them both said, "Good boys." I asked him if it was safe to step out. He assured me that it was.

Jason's sister came down and out the front door running toward him. She jumped into his arms and I could tell that they had a great relationship. She said, "Damn brother, how long has it been?" He replied, "Two years." Jason introduced me to her as Susan. Susan told us to come in and eat. We agreed. While feasting on fried chicken, mashed potatoes, and green beans, Susan and Jason spoke of their dad. She told Jason that his condition had progressed rapidly and that his mind had deteriorated quite a bit. She told us where he was located.

After finishing what was the finest meal I had eaten in years, I thanked Susan. Jason told her that he felt compelled to go and see his dad and we were going there. They hugged and she asked Jason, "Will you be coming back?" He told her, "You know me. I'm kind of just drifting at the moment." She told him not to drift too far as we drove off.

Nearing the nursing home I could tell that Jason was getting a little nervous. I asked him if I should accompany him. He said he would like that. We walked into the front door and found the receptionist. The receptionist guided us down a long hallway that gave way to a nursing station. The nursing station was position so that anyone sitting behind the long curved desk could see down three hallways named A, B, and C. There was a hallway named "D" but it was behind closed doors. Jason gave the nurse behind the desk his information. She told him that he could find his dad in "D" hall just beyond the closed doors. Jason looked at me and said, "Wish me luck," and I did.

As Jason walked through the doorway, I inquired to the nurse as to why D hall had closed doors. She told me that it was the Alzheimer's hall and that it was easier to control the ambulatory Alzheimer's patients by containing them somewhat.

While waiting for Jason, I couldn't help but notice that my Spirit Guide was nowhere to be found. I guess there was nothing for this vigilante to do here but wait around for my friend. I took a seat near the nurse station and began to notice the elderly people who were around. One elderly lady was in a wheel chair but could move the chair by using her feet. She came rolling by me and asked me if I had any cookies. I humored her by patting my pockets and saying, "I'm fresh out." She said, "That's ok, I know where these damn nurses hide them. Would you be my look out while I snag a few?" I was surprised at the cunning awareness the woman had and could not resist the comical events that was sure to transpire. I grabbed the back of her wheel chair and began to push her. I asked her where to go. She told me that just past "D" hall there was a kitchen. We strolled down to the entrance of the kitchen and she told me to just wait out in the hall as a look out. So I did. She rolled herself, using the pulling motion of her feet, into the kitchen. Before I had a chance to blink she came rolling back out as if she had just robbed a bank and said, "Hall ass!" I grabbed the handles of her chair and tilted her back to lift her feet off the ground and rode that wheelie swiftly back to "A" hall. She was holding in her lap an entire pack of chocolate chip cookies. We were both laughing at the fun we just had. She looked up at me and said, "Your cut is five cookies." "Cool," I said, "five is my lucky number." She asked me to roll her down to her room. I did. At the entrance she started coughing and asked me to help her lie down. I picked her up and laid her on her bed. She started coughing uncontrollably and I started to worry. I ran down to the nurse station and told the nurse there that the woman in room A25 needed some assistance. The nurse looked at me and said, "Are you sure it's room A25?" I said, "Certainly." I ran back to the room only to find it completely empty. The nurse was right behind me. I said, "I don't understand. She was right here." The nurse asked if the lady liked chocolate chip cookies. I told her the story and she looked at me and said, "You must have the sight." I asked, "What do you mean?" She explained the lady that used to occupy room A25 died two weeks ago. The nurse's description of her was right on. The nurse told me that I had a gift and to not let it freak me out. She went about her business and I had to sit down for a minute and let this all sink in.

I thought to myself, not only do I see the spirit of a warrior brave and accept his possessing guidance, but now I'm seeing ghosts! I surely must be nuts. Just then I heard someone say, "Not nuts, just blessed." Looking up I could see that the words came from an elderly man that had been sleeping in his geriatric chair. I asked him, "Did you just read my thoughts?" There was no reply and the man went back to his nap. Woe, I thought, I got to walk this off.

Walking back toward the way we came in, I soon realized that the layout of the building was such that there was an identical nurse station at the opposite end. The hallway that joined the two stations was paralleled by another in such a way that I could do laps like a track star around a small football field. After making a few laps, I decided to revisit the room where I apparently saw a ghost. While making my way down "A" hall I heard the terrible noises of someone who was obviously in bad shape and probably on their death bed. I notice a man about my age at the end of the hall. He was posting something up on the bulletin board. I walked down to the board as he left and saw a poem that had the lyrics of yet another Clifton Dee song. The title was "Terminal" and it read,

Look at me now.
Shrunken, broken, and worn.
Please tell me how,
my life can be so torn.

Nothing to ponder but my longing for death,
Gasping, hoping for my next and last breath.

Look at me now.
Don't turn away.
Respect me somehow.
This might be you someday.

Just as I was taking this all in, Jason found me and said, "Let's go Bro." I told him, "Yeah man, I'm starting to freak out a little."

We made our way back to the car. I asked Jason, "Where to now?" He said that he felt that he needed to stay in Montgomery for awhile. I told him that my journey would not be the same without him. He apologized for not being able to explore further with his new found friend but that perhaps when the time was right he would rejoin me. I gave him the information on how to find me in New Mexico and told him to look me up. He assured me he would. I drove him back to the rural two story house and we parted ways.

I had a lot to think about and enough road and time to do it. I decided that my next stop would be Jackson, Mississippi and headed west.

Chapter 5

Jackson

Making my way west, I finally cross the state line into Mississippi. By looking at my atlas I could tell that Interstate Highway 20 covered quite a bit of ground. Finally, I thought, I will be on one highway for a long stretch. I could see that I-20 would lead me through Mississippi, Louisiana, and into Texas as far as Abilene.

While starting to relax my thoughts about the whole nursing home incident, I began to feel kind of hungry. I didn't know if there were any snacks in the glove box or not. I leaned over from my driving position and opened the glove box with my right hand. I almost jumped out of my seat when I saw five chocolate chip cookies. Woe, I thought. Am I just imagining things, or are these the cookies from my new elderly ghost friend? No matter, they taste pretty damn good! Smiling at my situation, I say out loud, "I'm blessed."

Time and distance passed by and eventually I was seeing road signs for Jackson, Mississippi. I figured it was time for some gas and pulled off the highway into a small outskirt community. There was a sign for gas with an arrow pointing south that followed a road called Redemption Avenue. I turned south under the overpass and headed to the gas station that was in view.

Pulling slowly up to the pumps, I could hear amazing sounds of a gospel choir bellowing from the small church across the street. I went into the station and saw an elderly black man smoking a pipe behind the register. I gave him the money for gas and asked him what kind of church was across the street. He pulled his pipe from his lips, smiled, and said, "That church, my friend, is the kind that will change your life." "Is it non denominational?" I inquired. "That church is open to anyone seeking enlightenment," he stated with a grin. I thanked him for the gas and walked outside.

It was a beautiful Wednesday evening and I had nothing much to do except figure out where to sleep for the night. I decided to go visit the church and have a little look. As I approached the steps that led up to the beautiful stained glass doors, I hesitated a bit. I remembered the last time I had been to a service. It was when I was 15 years old and the turmoil of home life was about to come to full awareness. My twisted father was leading the service as he often did in the absence of the pastor. I remember thinking, what an interesting acting job he does. He had all the people of the congregation believing that he was a righteous man. Shit, I thought, far freakin from it! As I came closer to reaching the top of the stairs I realized that it had been ten years since I stepped foot in a house of worship.

As I slowly opened the large stained glass door, the sounds of the choir were getting louder. I stepped inside and was witness to one of the most glorious displays of praise I had ever seen. The congregation was entirely made up of Black folks all dressed in beautiful clothing. The choir was uniformly dressed in shiny black and red robes that swayed with them as they clapped in unison and stepped with the rhythm. I could not only see the wonderful expression of praise but also feel the soulful, joyous, and spiritual exertion. The song they were singing was an old gospel hymn that I remembered as a kid. I did not remember it ever sounding nearly this good.

The song gave way to a glorious solo sang by the leader. Then the same person made her way to the podium. I could tell at that point that she was also the pastor. The sign outside read, "Led by Pastor Shirley Ann." She wiped the sweat from her brow and took a few minutes to let all the excitement of the praise subside a little. She began to share some words of guidance and wisdom with the congregation. She started talking about the things that will manifest abundance in your life. One thing she conveyed is the fact that a gratitude attitude will win you favor in the eyes of the lord. She said that if a person never learns to be happy with what they all ready have then why would the spirit of the Lord see fit to bless them with more. "For instance," she said, "If you have a house that is in need of repair, do you wish on another house or do you take the steps necessary to nurture and bless the house you already have?" She said that she moved into a house 5 years ago that was falling apart. She said she bought it for nothing more than the taxes owed. "Now, 5 years later the tax man is telling me that my house is worth 5 times the amount

I paid for it." She paused to let it sink in. "I'm not here to give you real estate advice. I'm just telling you that I had a gratitude attitude the entire time and thanked the Lord Jesus that I at least had a roof over my head and to give me the strength to improve what is already mine." She referenced the story of Job and how he had everything stripped from him yet he still gave thanks and praise to the Lord and eventually received everything back plus more. In her closing statement she said, "If you want more, then be thankful for what you already have."

I could see that she was absolutely filled with the spirit. Her character was strong enough to demand respect from even the toughest of men yet there was a kindness in her eyes that was extremely inviting. She gave a word of prayer full of gratitude then dismissed the congregation. The people all stood and started to make their way out. I stood there at the back of the church in complete awe of the entire event. I could not believe that a service could ever leave a person feeling this good. As the people passed by on their way out, I did not feel out of place even though I was the only white person here. They just smiled and nodded hellos as they made their way outside. The pastor was the last one to follow the crowd. I stepped outside just before she did and stood at the top of the stairs. Upon her exit the sun was just beginning to set and as she turned to face me it made a stunning glowing circle that surrounded her. The gas lanterns that hung from each side of the entrance had a counter glow that softly lit up her face. I thought, wow, I am surely in the presence of an angle. I didn't say a word. She looked at me and said, "Do not worry. You are on the righteous path. I can see it. You will soon find peace and be at rest but you know that the work the Lord has for you is still not complete." She said, "Bless you child for doing the work that no one else can do." She took my face with both of her hands and kissed my forehead.

With nothing else to say, I seemed to float back to my car. I thought what a beautiful night and how cool it would be to sleep outside on this summer's eve. I went back into the gas station to ask the man where I could buy a small tent and some camping gear. He said that he had been holding on to some gear for someone just like me. I ask him how much he wanted for it. He said in a joyful voice, "Any man that comes out of that church glowing like you, can have whatever he wants free of charge." I asked him, "What do you mean?" He said, "Man, you look like Moses when he came down from the mountain." I just laughed and accepted his kind offer. I asked the man if there was anywhere to camp close to the Interstate. He told me that about 5 miles west on I-20 there was an exit for a dirt road named Solitude and that 5 miles south on that road was some camping grounds. Thanking him for his hospitality, I grabbed the gear and jumped into the Caddy.

It was now getting dark and I still felt surreal from the church event. I turned onto Solitude Road and thought of how tired I was getting. I thought perhaps after setting camp, I would slumber like the dead. I finally arrived at an area that had abandoned campfire pits and thought, this must be the place. I pulled over and left my headlights on so I could see. The area that I chose was at the base of an elongated hill that was covered in trees and brush. Just as I wondered what might be on the other side of the hill; I heard the cracking sound of a whip. At that moment I also heard the sounds of a wooden flute, the wind picked up, and I saw my guide standing in the distance. "There you are," I said out loud. He didn't seem to be on the war path but just standing there with his arms crossed and the look of contemplation as he stared up at the hill. I knew at that moment it was time for me to investigate.

I climbed up the mound while clinging to trees and brush as the incline was very steep. Upon nearing the top, I slowed to a crawl to peek over and investigate what was on the other side. There was a glow coming from a campfire and a pickup. Holding a whip in one hand and a gun in the other was a scruffy looking white guy. He had stringy light colored hair and looked a little drunk. He was circling another man of a darker complexion whose hands and feet were bound by duct tape. The captive man was on his knees in a bent over position and had duct tape across his mouth.

Still circling his prey, the white guy was spouting racial slurs and cracking his whip as to intimidate his prisoner. I heard him say, "So you think you can come to my town, my bar, and hit on my women? You're a stupid spick!" Hearing this made my blood boil. I have zero tolerance for prejudice assholes like this one. Now Asshole will be his new name. Asshole squatted down to take a seat on a tree stump. He put down the whip to reach for his beer. I knew that I had to do something and remembered how I still had the gun I took from Baldy. I quickly slid down the hillside and retrieved the pistol from under the driver's seat of the Caddy.

After making my way back up the steep embankment, I peered again over the top and down on the scene. I was lucky that Asshole was setting on the other side of the fire so that the glare in his eyes would provide me with some cover. It was also a good thing that I liked to dress in all black. I slowly made my way down the hill and silently crept around and about 20 feet behind him. The prisoner could see me and I motioned finger to lips to be quite. At about 10 feet from him, I pulled back the hammer on the revolver and it made that unmistakable sound. I said, "Drop your gun." Asshole knew I had the upper hand and did as I suggested. I asked him to grab the duct tape that was on a nearby rock. I told him to get down on his knees and start wrapping the tape around one hand. After several spins around the one hand I told him to put his hands together as if to pray. He did and with one hand pointing the gun at his head I took the other and continued wrapping his hands together.

After feeling like Asshole was bound pretty well I stuffed my gun into the back of my pants and kicked him onto his side. I then duct taped his legs together all the way up to his knees. He started to beg a little and in a whiny voice said, "I wasn't going to hurt him. I was just trying to scare him." I stated, "I've heard enough out of your idiotic mouth." I grabbed the tape and started to wind it over his mouth and around his head. The Asshole was still making an effort to mumble something and I pushed him back to the ground.

"Now let's hear what you have to say," I said as I approached the captive man. I pulled the tape from his mouth as quickly as I could. He exclaimed, "Damn, thank you! I thought this asshole was gonna kill me."

He told me his name was Mario and that he was just in Jackson on business. Mario was apparently a descendant of the Native Americas and Spanish. He went on to tell me that as a salesperson it was common to take clients out for drinks and that was what led him to a bar named The Muskrat. I laughed, pointed toward Asshole, and said, "Looks like you found one." "I guess so," he replied. Mario told me that it was all going well until his client had to go and he decided to have a few more before returning to his hotel. While sitting by himself, a very attractive waitress was providing him beer and a little conversation. All the while Asshole was shooting pool and looking very agitated. Mario said he finally left the bar and before he could enter his car someone hit him from behind. "And now here we are," he said.

Feeling more relaxed at the thought of Mario just being an innocent bystander, I continued to help him cut the duct tape from his arms and legs. He thanked me as he stood and made his way to stand over Asshole. I told Mario that whatever he was thinking, we had all night and we should contemplate Asshole's punishment. He agreed and came back over to me sitting by the fire.

I got up to search Asshole's pickup. I found nothing but a full ice chest of beer, some rope, and a bag of beef jerky. I asked Mario if he was in a hurry to resume his journey. He told me that as strange as it might sound, he thought it might be nice just to sit by the fire for a while and enjoy the night air. I told him that it didn't sound strange at all. "Besides," I said, "we have a full chest of beer and some introduction conversation that I am dying to partake!" He laughed at my obvious optimism and agreed to hang out a bit.

Mario kept looking over at the prejudice asshole and I said, "Don't you worry, he's not going anywhere and I'm sure we will figure out what to do with him. Besides, maybe hearing some real men talk, he might learn something." Mario seemed to relax a little more as I did my best to let him know that I was a fair person and didn't harbor any racial hatred.

We both reached in the cooler for a cold one and upon popping the top, Mario held up his can in toasting fashion and said, "Salud." I returned his gesture. He told me about his family. He had a wife in Amarillo, TX and 3 girls. I said, "You got your hands full." He replied, "You don't even know man. Even the dog is a female." We laughed. I could tell by the way he spoke of his family that he was dedicated to providing them with everything. He told me how he was very driven to work as hard as he could in order to give his daughters more than he ever had as a child.

I told Mario of my journey across the states to my old stomping grounds in New Mexico. He asked me, "How is it that a white boy comes to the rescue of a man like me?" I looked him in the eyes and said, "I look at all men as equal until they prove otherwise. For instance, look at Asshole over there, he has definitely proven otherwise. Hence his new name, Asshole."

I reached into the cooler and in my best Spanish tongue roll I asked Mario, "Que es Otro?" Which means, do you want another? He looked at me and said, "Are you sure you're not Spanish?" I told him that I was predominantly of English descent but I'm sure there was a chili pepper in the mix somewhere along the way. We laughed some more. We talked more about racial categorization. I told him that I really didn't like to use the word

Hispanic in reference to a people who are a complex mix of native tribes in North, Central, and South America intermingled with settlement of people from Spain. I told Mario, "Rather than even try to label anyone I think we should just all be referenced as human." With the nectar of alcohol massaging my mind, I knew we were in for a night of deep philosophical conversation. And so it was.

Before I knew it we had talked the night almost into day. Mario asked, "What are we going to do with Asshole over there?" I told him that I thought the punishment should fit the crime so he definitely needed a knot on his head to match yours. Before I could even finish my sentence Mario had trotted over to Asshole and landed a kick to his face that would make the NFL proud. Blood splashed from Asshole's nose and made an interesting contrast on the nearby white flowers. "OK, what next?" Mario asked. "Well," I said, "I think he needs to learn a little humility. We should strip him naked and hang him by the waist from an over pass back east on I-20 and Redemption Avenue. We both laughed at the irony.

After stripping the fool of his clothes we stuffed him into the trunk of my Caddy. He was trying to scream through the duct tape and was so apparently terrified of the whole notion that I knew justice was right on.

We jumped into the Caddy with enthusiasm. It was about 4:30 a.m. and hopefully we could pull this off without being seen. We made our way east on 1-20 for 5 miles and parked the car. To our advantage, there wasn't a car in sight. The rope I had found in Asshole's pick up served us well as we swiftly tied one end around his waist and the other to the guard rail. As Mario effortlessly tossed Asshole over the side he exclaimed, "See you later Asshole!"

I felt that the scene needed a little more effect so quickly I remembered the can of spray paint in the trunk. I grabbed it and was able to go over the guard rail while standing on a ledge below that was the bottom of a 5 foot wide steel beam. It would serve well as a bill board. I wrote without hesitation in big bold red letters, "Prejudice Asshole."

I told Mario we should drive down and around to get the full effect. We jumped into the Caddy and made our way to the gas station I visited earlier. We turned around by the pumps and drove toward the swinging, naked, prejudiced asshole. It was such a funny site that Mario and I could not stop laughing. Mario said, "Look at that stupid piñata." Asshole was twitching about in utter disgrace and humiliation. I had a momentary vision of the man from the gas station looking at the spectacle and stating to me, "You go Boy."

Laughing our way back onto the highway and heading west, I looked at Mario and gladly stated, "Justice is served." He agreed and we made our way back to the campsite to pick up my gear.

I folded up the tent and quickly put everything away. I suggested to Mario that we leave this area of Mississippi immediately. He agreed and asked me to take him to his car that was back at The Muskrat Bar. As we drove up to his car, the sun was barely starting to shed some light. Mario shook my hand and thanked me. "My pleasure," I said. He told me that if I was ever in Amarillo to look him up. He said that he should be there because his traveling sales days are over. I assured him that I would keep that in mind. We shook hands again and he said, "Bueno." Mario jumped into his car and we both drove off.

Recalling all of the interesting turn of events that happened around Jackson, I smile. I wonder about my new friend Mario and his family. I realized in our short encounter that he was a good family man and was very amazed as I turned on the stereo to hear the D.J. announce, "Yet another song from the new artist Clifton Dee." The song was a live acoustical recording supported by an applauding audience. With the somber sounds of a cello accompanied by guitar, the artist gave a short introduction to his song titled "A Real Man."

A real man does not allow himself to
become confused or swallowed up by
the immorality and overwhelming chaos of today's society.

A real man looks at his would be enemies and smiles at them,
Not ever lowering himself to their crumbling levels of shame.

A real man feels pity for the lost minds that cannot find the
inner peace, love, and joy that dwells in the undying soul of
a real man.

Chapter 6

Shreveport

Trying with the best of efforts to stay awake, I crank up the stereo, roll down the windows, and lay onto the accelerator. While picking up speed, I can feel a second wind coming on and no longer feel as if I had been awake for 24 hours. The beautiful summer morning has come to greet me with an air of gratification. I can sense the presence of brotherhood from my new found friends even though they are on their own current journeys. I feel comfort in the fact that I have found friendship along these United States and have a little back up should my journey call for it.

If everything goes according to plan then my next stop should be Shreveport, Louisiana. Looking at the Atlas I can see that it is almost on the Texas, Louisiana border. I-20 has been serving me well and I hope that as I start to speed up even more that I don't encounter any police men. I decide to see just how fast the Caddy will go and floor it all the way. To my excitement the acceleration threw me back a little in the seat even though I was already going 75 MPH. The speedometer had the highest number as 125 MPH and that is where I decided to ease off the peddle. Cool, I thought, this old beast can actually move.

Finally after what seemed to be a relatively short period of time, I see signs for Shreveport. I would be making my approach to the city limits in about 5 miles. I thought at this point that I had survived on adrenaline long enough and it was time to get some real sleep. At the first sign of a hotel, I pulled off the highway and steered directly into the parking lot of what seemed to be a fairly nice one. It had an indoor pool and a sports bar.

Walking up to the front desk, I could tell that my mind and body was in dire need of some rest. I paid the person for one night. I asked if I could be on the first floor because I didn't have the strength to make it much further. I was given the key to room 105. I looked at the number and smiled again at the coincidental numeric luck while thinking, I must get some rest for I feel that there might be another story brewing right here in this hotel.

My room was directly in front of the indoor swimming pool. I knew that after my slumber it would be invigorating to jump right into the pool. How cool is that? I thought. I opened the door to room 105, walked exhaustingly to the bed and plopped my weary body right down. I looked at the clock and saw that it was only 1:00 p.m. As I knew it would, sleep came to me swiftly. Soon I started to have those dreams that come when you have been practically dead to the world for hours.

The first really bizarre dream started with me having the ability to fly. I especially enjoy my flying slumbers. Soaring about, I find myself landing on a busy city street with people everywhere who seem to be in an extreme rush. I get bumped by a strange man who is wearing a T-shirt and jeans. The man turns to me and asks if I have a problem. I reply, "No problem." Another man wearing his Sunday's best three piece suit turns and states, "I think he does have a problem." Both men in my dream begin to circle me as if to intimidate. The T-shirt guy says, "He thinks he's better than us." The suit wearer says, "He would love to tarnish our good name." Suit guy makes a lung at me and with no hesitation I reach down and grab him by his ankles and begin to swing him like a bat. Dreams are cool like that. Not only can I fly but I have super human strength. While swinging Suit man in pick ax fashion, I decide to end his existence by slamming his head to the pavement. His skull cracked open like a melon revealing that the only thing inside was nothing but dust. T-shirt guy got extremely frightened by the whole event and ran screaming like a little bitch. At this point in the dream I awoke feeling a little weird from the spectacle in my mind. I looked at the clock and it read 1:00 a.m. I could not believe that I had been asleep for 12 hours already. What was more unbelievable is the fact that I could sleep some more and so I did.

The next dream was just as bizarre as the first but in a more relaxing manner. Still with the ability to fly, I soar over the top of a grassy valley that has a stream running through it. Down below I see a long wooden table. I land to take a closer look. The table is loaded with every food imaginable. It is a feast fit for a king. Just as I sit to partake of the feast I hear a scream. The scream wasn't in my dream but one that woke me from it. I ran to the window and looked out toward the pool. It wasn't a scream of despair but one of delight as kids played freely in the pool.

I wondered how long I had been asleep. The clock on the night stand read 11:00 a.m. I could not believe how long I had slept. 22 hours? Could that be correct? I guess so because at that time the phone rang and it was the front desk clerk asking me if I wanted to pay for another day. I told him yes and that I would be right there.

With only my T-shirt and some shorts on I walked bare foot, billfold in hand, down to the front desk. The clerk asked how he could help me and I told him that I wish to pay for one more night. I asked him if there was a laundry room for I was in desperate need of some fresh clothes. He said that just around the corner from my room there was one. I thanked him and returning to my room I could see the children having their fun in the pool. I thought what the hell and said, "Banzai!" I jumped in great cannon ball fashion and landed in the middle of the pool with a splash that was sure to impress the young ones. Dripping wet I pulled myself out of the pool. Some of the children were saying, "Do it again." I replied, "Maybe later."

Feeling very rested and invigorated by my dip into the pool, I knew that I was ready for anything, even if anything meant the mundane task of chores. Opening my suit case, I put on my last pair of semi clean shorts and without a shirt made my way to the laundry room. There were coin operated machines and non coin operated ones with an attendee that asked, "Would you prefer doing your laundry yourself or shall I do them for you?" I said with a smile, "I think that it would be best for me to air out my own dirty laundry, if you know what I mean." The laundry attendant smiled as if she realized my attempt at metaphorical whit. She was a very attractive woman with mocha skin and a ruby smile. She looked to be about my age of 25. I worked the change machine for some quarters and began to purchase some detergent from another machine. The detergent machine took my money and wouldn't dispense my box. I started to hit the machine a little when the laundry attendant came over, put her hand on my shoulder and said in a soft voice, "You can use mine." I turned and looked at her. She was so obviously flirting in a great harlot manner. She knew exactly how to look and walk in order to seduce her prey. In my experiences I had the misfortune to encounter women such as this. An inexperienced lad would probably fall right into her web. A few years earlier, I know I would have for she is very beautiful. Without saying a word she moves with all the right curves and could glance at a man as if to mesmerize him to the point of being a drooling dumfounded idiot. Yep, I thought, this is the girl that your mommas warned you about. Knowing that she was nothing but trouble I told her, "Thanks for the offer but I shall have to pass." About that time, as if fate agreed with my decision, the detergent box in the machine fell. Cool, I thought, no need to use hers.

I threw in a load of colors and whites in separate machines. The attendant looked at me and said, "Is that all you wear, black and white?" I smiled politely and said, "As far as the naked eye can tell, but on the inside there are so many shades of grey it makes for a complicated personality." By this time I could tell that she was losing interest in my attempts of metaphoric conversation and went back to her work. I returned to my room for a much needed shower and shave.

After a steaming hot shower I stood in front of the mirror and thought of how liberating my new hair style has become. All I do for a cut is open up my hair clipper case, pop on a one guard, and commence to working the clippers back and forth all around my head. Cost effective and practical. There is no combing or worrying about the hairdo. As far as facial hair is concerned, I change it up all the time. Currently choosing to not have any facial hair, I quickly shave my face clean and return to the laundry room to put my clothes in the dryer.

Returning to my room to wait for my clothes to be finished, I began to feel hungry. This hotel actually has room service, I thought as I saw a pamphlet on the desk. I called the room service number and requested the juiciest, thickest, and medium rare burger they could bring me. The service member asked me, "Would you like some fries?" I replied, "No, just a side of whiskey with a beer chaser." Not expecting that they would accommodate my last request, the waiter said, "House whiskey or not." "Cool, I'll take the house blend and a domestic beer." The person told me it would be about 20 minutes.

As I finished my last bite, I thought, how excellent that burger was. It ranked up there about number two. The number one burger in my opinion was those of my Aunt's at Old West Burgers in Artesia. This thought brought me to another, Keisha. I wondered what she was doing and remembered the restaurant name her aunt owned, Big Beef. I tried to shake off my thoughts of her as I shot down the whiskey and took a drink of my beer.

By now I knew for sure my clothes would be ready and so they were. I folded them neatly into the suitcase. Laughing to myself, I thought, what should I wear? The humor lies in the fact that I had 7 pairs of the exact same thing. I had seven black T-shirts, seven black pairs of jeans, and seven black pairs of boxer briefs. The only whites that I had were the seven pair of socks.

I got dressed and finished off the ensemble with a black pair of high lace up steel toe biker boots. Looking in the mirror, I thought, should I tuck the shirt or not? Sure, why not. This gave me the opportunity to show off my new black belt with a silver buckle shaped like a hand with the middle finger gesture. Now for my final piece I shall adorn my neck with the bone and bead necklace given to me by my departed Grandfather.

Feeling refreshed and well rested, I decided to explore the hotel a little and see what stories it had to offer. I walked outside my room where children were still splashing and having a good time in the pool. The pool was surrounded by a simulated stream that actually had real gold fish in it. There were fake bushes and trees that added to the river like atmosphere. The roof above the pool was three floors high and let in a little sun light. The elevators had glass so that a person could see out into the pool area and as the elevator made its escape to the higher floors a person could see outside all the way to the final 10th floor.

The west side of the hotel was all one story and had a restaurant/ sports bar and some convention rooms. I decided to set at the bar awhile and have another beer. I approached the bar two stools down from a man who was watching the TV and cussing quite comically. The event he was watching was highlights of the last Dallas vs. Washington football game. "Those sick San Antonios," was one of replies as he watched Dallas score a touchdown. According to his remarks as he watched the game, I could tell that he was a fan of Washington. I thought it was kind of rare in this neck of the woods for someone to be cheering for that team. He too was of the same descending ancestry as my latest friend Mario. By that I mean he seemed to be of the Native Americas mixed with Spanish tongue and blood. The bar tender seemed to be amused by the Washington fan and kept him in a steady supply of beer. I asked the bar tender for one and began to watch the highlight reel. I said out loud, "How about them boys?" The Washington fan looked at me and said, "You're not a sick San Antonio too, are you?" I told him that it all depends on what he means by that. He told me that he was a fairly new father and that in an effort to keep his language clean around his 3 yr old son he had to start using different phrasing for cuss words. "For example," he said, "San Antonio has taken the place of Son of a Bitch. You can use it in many different ways. Not only do I say sick San Antonio but also use it in exclamation such as San Antonio Texas!"

I changed the subject and asked him if he liked draft beer. He said, "I like any beer that sits in front of me." I laughed at his beer drinking optimism. I asked the bar tender for a pitcher of beer and two mugs. Holding out my hand, I introduced myself. "I'm Tristan." He shook my hand and said, "I'm L.B." I asked him what L.B. stood for and he just smiled and said, "Right now it stands for Liquor and Beer." I laughed and asked the bar tender to add 2 shots of tequila to the order. We raised the shots in the air to toast and L.B. said, "Salud."

About 30 minutes went by and we began to loosen up a bit. L.B. started to tell me about his son and how the mother of his child was really up to no good. Her name was Margarita and that she was from San Antonio and that is where they met. That gave a whole new meaning to his new cuss words. I asked him what brought him to Shreveport. He told me that the mother of his son had a certain addiction to meth and that she didn't always think very clearly. He said that she sometimes exhibited some very bizarre motives. She had met up with some dealer who convinced her to move to Shreveport. "As a matter of fact," he said, "she is a laundry maid right here in this hotel." Right away I knew he was talking about the maid that I had encountered while doing my laundry. He went on to tell me that he was just in town to figure out a way to get his son and be done with the She Devil once and for all.

He told me that he found out that she had started to date a prominent figure in Shreveport. Her latest victim was a widower who gained public respect as a principle for one of the local High Schools. This man's name was Ben. Ben was now running for Mayor and would be holding an election campaign party and press conference right here in this hotel tonight. L.B. told me that he also found out that Margarita was still dating the meth dealer and they both had some really shady plans for Ben the principle soon to be Mayor. L.B.'s sources also told him that Margarita had Ben so wrapped around her little finger that he was blind to the whole black widow scenario. L.B. said, "She's a crafty Bitch."

I asked L.B. what his plan was and he told me he wasn't quite sure. My wheels started spinning and I asked him if he would like my help. He said, "I'll take all the help I can get." I told L.B. that by watching an old movie about Vegas I learned that if you want anything at all in a hotel, all you have to do is grease the palms of the Bellmen. I asked him if he had a little palm greasing money. He said he had been saving for just such an occasion. "Ok," I said, "here's the plan."

I told him that we needed one good Bellman on board so we went to the front desk. Close to the front doors there was a Bell stand and a Bellman ready to help us as we approached. Upon my introduction to him I palmed him a 20 dollar bill and said, "My name is Tristan and we sure could use your help." He said his name was Jeremy and replied, "Whatever you need sir." I told him to call me Tristan and introduced him to L.B. I asked Jeremy to accompany us to my room and he agreed.

Upon entering the room Jeremy asked, "Do you need me to carry some luggage?" I replied, "I'm afraid our request is going to be a little more complex than that." I told him that we are working on a plan to publicly out Margarita as the money hungry meth head that she is. Jeremy said, "The laundry girl?" I said, "That woman is all kinds of trouble. My new friend here just wants his son back and for her to be exposed for the conniving woman she is." Jeremy said, "Sounds interesting to me but time is money." I asked him how much he averaged a day in tips. He said that he usually made around $200. Without hesitation, L.B. said, "Here's $250. Are you in?" "In like Flynn." Jeremy replied.

I asked Jeremy what time the press conference was going to take place. He said that the hotel expected Ben to show up around 5:00 p.m. The conference was to take place in the main conference hall about 6:00 p.m. I told Jeremy that I needed a suit and something that would pass for a press camera. He said that I was in luck because someone had left a black suit behind that was about my size. They were supposed to send it to the owner that day but he forgot. Jeremy said that I must be the luckiest guy on earth because there was also a video camera left by another guest that same day. I looked at both Jeremy and L.B. and said with a smile, "Yeah, I'm blessed."

"O.K.," I said, "it's 4:00 p.m. now so that gives us an hour to rehearse." "What do you mean rehearse?" L.B. replied. I told them that we were going to put on one hell of a show. I was going to pose as a local news reporter while Jeremy posed as my camera man. I told L.B. that he should just be himself and that we would corral Ben to him in the bar. "You just share with him what you know about Margarita. We will follow up by confronting him after your conversation with some press questions that will surely send him running far away from the She Devil. He can thank us later for saving his career."

"The other thing we need to do is make sure that Margarita is caught red handed with some meth with the intention to distribute. That ought to land her some much needed time in prison. Maybe there she would have time to realize the error of her ways." Jeremy said that he had seen Margarita frequently visit a room on the 9th floor, room 903. He remembered the name of the guest. Mr. Montez. L.B. said, "Does he have a tattoo of a naked woman on his forearm?" Jeremy replied, "Yes he does." L.B. said that was the meth dealer that was aiding in the destruction of his life. Jeremy said that he did notice Margarita visiting the room quite often but she never stayed long. It was as if she was his runner. I smiled and said, "This is going to be like shooting fish in a barrel."

I told Jeremy to do his best to convince Margarita that he was in desperate need of some meth and have her agree to meet him in the laundry room about 5:30 p.m. I told him to meet me at the front entrance ready to act as my camera guy about 4:50 I told L.B. to set at the bar and just be himself. I asked Jeremy if he could recruit another Bellman just to get Ben to set next to L.B. in the bar. He said he probably could but how was the Bellman to do it. I told him to tell his helper to escort Ben upon arrival to the bar telling him that there was a complimentary drink provided by the hotel in order to loosen him up for his big night. As if we were a football team on the verge of the greatest play of our careers, I told them to put their hands in. "On three, everybody say justice! One, two, three," we all said, "Justice!"

4:50 rolled around and I stood at the front entrance. Looking at myself in the reflection of the windows, I could tell that the borrowed suit fit me perfectly. Jeremy was right on time with camera in tow. I asked him how it went with Margarita. He said that it went perfect and that she agreed to meet him in the laundry room at 5:30. Jeremy said that he knew a narcotics officer and that we should call on him at that time. I agreed and felt very pleased with our own craftiness and apparent blessings.

Just as we thought we would have a few more minutes to contemplate our plan, Ben showed up. I looked at Jeremy and said, "Game on." Upon entering the hotel the other Bellman greeted Ben and escorted him to the bar and motioned for him to set next to L.B. The Bellman explained the compliments of the hotel and ordered Ben a drink. Jeremy and I were watching as L.B. seamlessly began to speak to Ben. "What brings you here?" L.B. asked Ben. "It's a breakthrough night for me," said Ben. "Yeah I know about breakthroughs. I had a woman breakthrough my pants and give me the nastiest case of herpes. The doctors say I'm lucky I still have a penis," L.B. said with a grin. "Sorry to hear that," replied Ben as he looked a little disturbed. L.B. went on to tell Ben his story of the meth head She Devil and how she worked right here in the hotel's Laundry Department. L.B. could tell that he now had the aspiring politician's undivided attention.

Ben asked, "What is her name?" L.B. said, "Margarita." With that unveiling truth, Ben got up and looking bewildered, began to exit the bar. Before he could get a few steps from his stool, Jeremy and I were there with a fake microphone in my hand and an empty camera in Jeremy's. I said without hesitation, "Mr. Principle, sir is it true that you are romantically involved with a well known meth dealer?" Looking very stunned, Ben said quickly, "No comment." I said, "Sir, how will this affect the election?" Ben said in true politician manner, "I have no Idea what you are talking about. I must go. That is all." Ben made his way quickly to the outer hall and into the conference room.

Jeremy, L.B., and I quickly made our way to my room. We were jumping up and down from the excitement. L.B. said, "That sick San Antonio will run from Margarita like a rabbit from the coyote." I said, "That was the plan but also to have a little fun in the process. Now if you will be so kind as to call your narcotics buddy, Jeremy, then the plan shall be complete." Jeremy made the call and with flawless execution the narcotics team arrived at 5:30 in the laundry room to find Margarita in possession of meth. The team also made their way to room 903 to find Mr. Montez and his operation. Jeremy, L.B. and I went out front to watch the whole spectacle unfold. We could hear cheers coming from Ben's conference. I thought how cool it was that we helped an innocent man dodge a bullet. At the same time as if it were all in slow motion, the cops were walking Margarita and Mr. Montez out. They were handcuffed and looking very angry. The cop cars drove away as another car showed up. L.B. said, "That looks like Margarita's mom." It was and with her was his son. Still with everything seeming to be in slow motion, L.B.'s son ran to him and jumped into his arms. Margarita's mom said that she was well aware of her daughter's shortcomings and that she had talked to social workers who said that the best place for the child was with his father. L.B. couldn't agree more and asked the grandmother if she could watch the little boy for a few moments while he thanked his new friend.

L.B. told me that if ever I was in San Antonio to look him up. I agreed and said, "Good luck." L.B. said that he had never found anyone so willing to be as helpful as myself especially upon just meeting. I told him with a smile, "That's what I do." He thanked me and with a solid hand shake said, "Until we meet again." The three of them got into the car and left. Jeremy looked at me and said, "I think it's time to have some more fun." I agreed and back into the bar we went.

After a few hours of drinks and laughs I decided it was time to return to my room for some sleep. I thanked Jeremy for a wonderful stay and made my way back to room 105. I lay down on the bed and thought of the whole day's events. I wondered when I should see my spirit guide again. Not that I was looking for a more accelerating justifying event, O.K. maybe I do look forward to those times. I wonder if that is a good or bad thing. I quickly fall asleep only to be awakened by the noises of kids in the pool. I look at the clock and it reads 11:00 a.m. Wow, I slept long again, only this time I had no dreams. I knew that I had to check out by 12:00 but I wanted to take one last dip in the pool.

I went out into the pool area with my swim trunks on and made a flying leap into the pool. The water felt very refreshing. I swam around a bit noticing the children as they played. There was one middle aged man in the pool who seemed a little odd. He was watching the children intently as they swam by him. He would reach out to touch the little girls as they swam. I could tell that the children were not with him as they looked at him with suspicious eyes. About that time I felt a cold chill go up my spine and saw my guide at the edge of the pool. My spirit guide was holding a hatchet over his head and threw it at the man in the pool. Being only a vision for me the hatchet seemed to disappear as it landed into the pool man's forehead. I decided to take a closer look. Being able to hold my breath would serve me well as I made my way under water from one end of the pool to his side. While under water I could see that the pervert was obviously excited by the young girls who played in the pool. The sick bastard was pleasuring himself with one hand while trying to reach out and touch the kids with the other. I popped up behind him to his surprise and said in a low calm voice, "Get your ass out of this pool." The perverts reply was the absolute wrong one when he said, "Screw you." I could hear my guide let out a yell and I drug the man down under the water. I was trying to be as nonchalant as I could to not frighten the children. While under the water it was impossible to land any punching blows so I had to improvise some punishment. The one thing that quickly entered my mind was to gouge out his eyes. So while the man was struggling to resurface I took both of my hands and wrapped them around his head. With my fingers cradling the back of his head I sunk both of my thumbs as deep as I could stand into his eye sockets. At the point of seemingly feeling his brains I released my grip. The sick bastard inhaled some water and started to look bleak. I pushed him to the pool steps and drug him out. About that time the man started to regain his faculties and began to put up a fight. I was done with this idiot and with one hand on his throat gave him a clothes line trip that sent his head slamming down on the hard cement floor. The sick bastard was out but still breathing. One of the nearby parents just noticing us asked what happened. I said, "He must have slipped." The parent asked if she should call the front desk or 911. I said, "Only if you wish."

I returned quickly to my room, grabbed my things, and headed out to the Caddy. By that time an ambulance had shown up. I thought, maybe that sick bastard will change his ways. I got into the Caddy and started heading west again on I-20. Wow, I thought, yet another interesting adventure. I thought of L.B. and his son. I remembered the very apparent love in his eyes as he spoke of his son. I remembered the perfect way they looked together as he carried his son off to put him in the car. How strangely coincidental, that the next song on the radio was so obviously fitting and by that new artist, Clifton Dee. It was a hard hitting song with a strong electric guitar intro that led to his lyrics of a song titled "My Blood."

You can choose and plan to be.
Recognize the root and the fruit of your tree.

Abundance my seed will bring.
Understanding the truth,
His praise, me and mine will sing.

Master mind of offspring installs in me eternal life.
Accept the struggle and the strife.

Clifton Dee

Pass my speech with greatness of wisdom.
With nourishing hand I will lend them,
these words as they think of me.
You can choose and plan to be.
Recognize the root and the fruit of your tree.

Walking blood I see.
He learns so fast, his persistence is keen.
Still it's up to me to make sure he's clean.

Nothing more bonding or bold,
for now his cards are in my hands.
It's up to me how it will unfold.

Training thought for love and wit.
His life keeps me going.
Because of him I will never quit.

Walking blood I see.
Second chance to make blood right,
Clay in my hands molding into flight.
Soaring blood I see.

Chapter 7

Artesia

I couldn't deny the absence of financial funding for my journey and thought to myself, I sure hope I make it through Texas into New Mexico. I knew that if I broke through the eastern border that most of my friends would not hesitate to come help me out if need be. This Caddy was quite the gas guzzler and I think I have enough money for one more tank and by my calculations that is about how much it's gonna take to get there. I might be riding into Artesia on fumes and a prayer but I bet I make it to my destination.

After about 6 hours on I-20 I can see signs for Abilene and think, finally, I'm at least halfway through Texas with about 6 hours to final destination. After reaching Abilene I knew that it was time to get off the Interstate Highway and head up to the U.S. highway 180. I stopped to fuel up at the next gas station. At this point it took everything I had to not head straight for Lubbock to find that woman that my heart ached so much to see. I knew that I had to overcome the urge to go and sweep her up and run far into the happily ever after. I knew that the only way I was going to be able to finally settle down is to take care of the punishing business in my birthplace. The beautiful Keisha was going to have to be an afterthought for me. I wondered how safe and interesting her jaunt across America was. I expect that it wasn't quite as eventful as mine. I thought of her 5 year old son Billy and wondered if he remembered my comment as to becoming friends.

With the chances of heading north to Lubbock fading and the eastern border of New Mexico growing near, I realized that Hobbs would be the first town I encounter in New Mexico. Upon approaching the state line I could see the welcome sign with the image of the New Mexico state flag. I have always admired the vibrant yellow flag with the blood red splashes that outlined the sun symbol. It has the intense qualities that lead to the ever truthful state phrase, "Land of Enchantment."

I think, Land of Enchantment indeed. I can start to feel my blood pumping just at the thought of finally being back in such a diversified geological area. My old stomping grounds have always kept me mystified. This state can lead you from some of the most amazing sand dunes coupled by a desert region to the most beautiful mountains imaginable and back again to desert all in one road trip heading west. Mother earth has seen fit to bless New Mexico with a playground for her child that never grows into a monotonous scene.

Feeling very exhilarated upon entering my home state, my heart begins to beat even faster. The wonderful country air couple by the adrenaline pumping into my system has me feeling as if I could fly. My spirit guide makes an appearance. He doesn't let out a war cry but is galloping on his horse as if he too is excited to be in this state. My ordeals with helping people to this point are starting to pale in comparison to my soon to be personal encounters. Now the vengefulness I feel in my heart is starting to slowly build with every passing mile and I can sense that my spirit guiding brave would shadow my every move.

Passing through Hobbs I caught a road leading to Loco Hills. By now I could hardly stand the intensity of being back in my place of birth. Ultimately I knew that after my retribution rages have ensued, I would not be able to ever return. Such a shame for I love the atmosphere that seems to consume my spirit and cries out in a primal invitation to join the circle of life in full bloom.

By now it is dark and nearing 10:00 p.m. on a wonderfully vibrant Saturday night. As I drive near to my home town I remember how you can actually smell it before you see it. Artesia has the Navajo refinery that is constantly churning out the crude oil into to finer stuff. A lot of the people will tell you that it smells like money. I say it smells like the degradation of a land and people from ancient years. Passing right by the monstrous labyrinth of pipe and smoke I finally reach First Street and wonder to myself, what now? I decided to take a chance on fate and remembered the bowling alley/bar that seemed to attract a crowd every now and then. I headed south to its location. Approaching the parking lot I could see that quite a few people must have decided to gather here on this Saturday night. I hoped that I would run into someone I knew.

Walking through the neon lit parking lot the excitement of being back in this small town lifts me up and brings a huge smile to my face. I enter the front of the bar and immediately a voice bellows out, "Tristan!" It was one of my best friends ever growing up. I replied, "Daniel, get your ass over here and let me hug your neck!" He had been sitting at a table surrounded by familiar faces. He practically ran up to me and lifted me off the ground in a bear hug that would make Yogi proud. It felt so good to be in the comfort of childhood friendship.

Daniel asked, "Where the hell have you been?" I told him of my seclusion under the ocean and how it was hard at times go get out any communication. He told me how glad he was that I was here and motioned me over to his table. Without the need for any introductions several people at the table came with hugs and handshakes. A few of the females were some that I had dated in junior high and high school. They were mostly paired with guys that I really knew little about. Then I saw the lone and beautiful Sarah. As she waited her turn at greeting me it was as if I could not hear anything and everything fell into slow motion. Sarah had eyes so terrifically grey that just one gaze would hold any man captive. She had the sad look of a woman in need of rescue but strangely enough was always the happiest person in the room. Her sense of humor kept everyone laughing in her presence. The very interesting thing about her as teenagers was that she notoriously had held on to her virginity. As she made her approach the glow around her would suggest that the purity of her soul was probably still intact. Still feeling like everything was in slow motion she made her way to me, wrapped her arms around me, and gave me a hug that turned me into an emotional whirl of yin and yang. It was if I could feel love and hate all at the same time. It was the strangest thing. The loving embrace felt as if we started to float when she whispered in my ear, "It is so good to have you back Tristan. Take care of business diligently and you shall soon have your peace." About that time as if being woken from a dream, Daniel was saying, "Dude, are you O.K.?" He was shaking me by the shoulders and brought me to the realization that I was only embracing myself. Shocked at the sudden absence of the angelic Sarah I asked Daniel, "Where did she go?" He asked, "Who?" I said, "Sarah." He seemed a bit confused and told me that I seemed to go into a trance and wrapped my arms around myself without answering to anyone for about a minute. I said, "But the beautiful grey eyed Sarah was just right here." Daniel said, "You mean fun loving untouchable Sarah?" "Precisely," I said. Daniel told me that she had passed away 2 years ago in a tragic car accident. He asked, "Dude, are you seeing ghosts again?" I told him "Well, I have a lot to tell you my good friend and we are going to need plenty of beer to get through these stories."

Daniel and I found a secluded bench seat area of the bar and sat down with a pitcher of beer and a couple of mugs. Daniel told me that he knew the waitress and she promised to keep us in a steady supply of the golden refreshment. I knew that I could trust my loyal friend and began to tell him everything that had happened on the road home. I told him how I felt driven with the assistance of my spirit guide to make a final punishing stand right here in this south eastern corner of New Mexico. Daniel knew everything of my twisted father and my upbringing. He also had heard of the tragic, senseless, and brutal murder of my

Grandfather. I could tell that Daniel was on board with my plans and still remained the happy go lucky friend I so desperately needed in this dark time. We finished off the hours with jokes and laughter. Daniel invited me to stay on his couch for the night. I agreed. He also suggested that he drive me there using my car. I agreed that mixing beer with visions of ghosts was probably not the ideal time to be behind the wheel. We made it safely to his place and without hesitation I promptly fell asleep on the couch.

The next morning I was awakened by the sounds of honking. I got off the couch and saw that it was my other fantastic childhood friend Jon. He was in his old mustang that he prized so much. I immediately ran to him and as he opened his door I tackled him as if to ruff him up. After laying him down in his front seat and giving him a few light punches in playful manner, I decided to give him a hug and let him out of the car. Jon is one of the most diverse characters I ever had the pleasure of knowing. He was always the big kid growing up. He was the meanest middle line backer on the football field. His diversity lies in the fact that not only does he have brute physical force to be reckoned with by any foe but he also has great musical talent. He can pick out anything and I mean anything on the guitar. There were times as a kid when I would sit in awe and listen to him play for hours.

I couldn't help but grab him again in a bear hug and say, "I've missed you; you barbaric, Viking looking, and race car having sick San Antonio!" He laughed and said, "What's a sick San Antonio?" I told him about my new friend from San Antonio and his efforts to clean up cuss words. He laughed again and asked if Daniel and I wanted to go for a good old fashion cruise. I replied, "Hell Yeah!"

We all piled into the old mustang with me in the back. Immediately Jon turned on some music and we were off. Our cruise started out on Main Street. There was a car hopping burger place that was ideal for a turn around. This was the place of congregation as teenagers, the place where most everything to know as a high school kid was announced by word of mouth. The ever important messages such as where the party for that night was going to take place. Our cruise would lead back down Main to a convenience store where another turn around would ensue. Back in our high school heyday's this would be referred to as "Dragging Main."

With one last drag of Main just as a walk down memory lane, Daniel said to me, "I really think there is someone you need to meet." I asked him who and he told me about his boss at the local butcher shop. He said that the man's name was Ralph and that he knew my Grandfather well. I agreed that I should meet with him and asked Jon to drop me off there. Daniel and Jon said they were gonna go and visit some other people and they would return in about an hour.

Upon entering the butcher shop I remembered this place as a kid. I thought of how cool it was that there is a stuffed long horn steer head mounted on the wall. Just as I remembered, toward the back rested the mounted head overlooking the cooler display of premium beef cuts. As I approached the counter a man came from behind a plastic curtain that led to the rear of the shop. He stopped in his tracks and looked at me. He said, "Son, you have the look of your Grandfather in your eyes." I said, "So, you know who I am." He told me that my Grandfather had spoke highly of all his grandchildren but that the adventurous Tristan shared his passion for life. Ralph told me that my Grandfather had left instructions with him to share as much information with me as possible in the event that I should seek it. Butcher Ralph told me to lock the front door and turn the sign to close because he and I had many things to discuss.

I did as he suggested and returned to the meat counter where he waved me back to follow him behind the plastic curtain. In the back was a table surrounded with four chairs. On the table was a wine bottle that had a candle stick which had melted around the top. Ralph lit the candle with a match and reached into the nearby refrigerator for a couple of beers. We sat at the table and cracked open our refreshments.

Ralph was a strong and lean looking man. He was basically sleeved with tattoos of various sorts. Although his countenance portrayed a stern existence, I soon found him to be charming and full of life. We talked about my journey to this point in my life and I felt confident that I could share with him my intentions to dish out some judge, jury, and pain for three remaining assholes. Ralph could not agree more. He told me some very interesting things about my Grandfather. One of which was the story of how my Grandfather decide to boot leg some hooch. I said, "You mean like moonshine." Ralph told me that the stuff my Grandfather would brew was some of the most interesting and talked about elixirs in all of New Mexico. Of course the talk would be amongst the secretive secluded conversations of people Grandpa trusted. Ralph said, "Your Grandfather told me that in every pint there was at least one drop of his sweat." He went on to tell me that Grandpa had made friends with a Navajo man that supplied him with a root. The root was the main distilling ingredient in the stiff drink he called Spirit Quest. Ralph said that he kept his operation at a minimum, selling only to a select few he trusted. Ralph went on to tell me that my Grandpa made the claim that any man who could finish a pint in one night and live to tell about it would have a guiding vision beyond belief. Ralph told me that my Grandpa was quite the adventurer and that if I continued to seek out people who knew and loved him that I was sure to stumble on some more terrific treasures. He stood from the table and walked over to a safe. He whirled the combination and popped it open. Reaching inside he said that he had been saving his last bottle of Spirit Quest for such a moment as this. He told me that we should only do one shot a piece and that I should reserve the rest for when I felt brave enough to attempt more. I thought to myself, little does he know but I'm gonna have my spirit quest tonight. He poured us each a shot and raised his hand to toast, "To Bruce!" We touched our shots together and tossed the elixir down our throats. Right away I knew what Ralph meant about being brave enough. The shot made its way down my throat with the burning sensation of the hottest pepper imaginable. As the liquid almost stole my breath, I could feel the mind altering affects immediately. Not unbearably but with one shot I instantly felt extremely surreal. Ralph looked at me and laughed saying, "Kinda grabs you don't it?" With trying to keep my pride in tack I replied, "A little." I reached for the bottle. It was just a regular pint sized narrow shaped whiskey bottle. Ralph said that my Grandpa had just a few bottles made that had a label. He told me that a local printer friend of his created the labels, one of which was on my bottle. I looked it over. It was a picture of what seemed to be the exact replica of my spirit guide; a warrior brave with a blood red hand print on one side of his face. His long jet black hair had a leather band holding it tightly against his head smartly parted down the middle. There were extensions of leather from the band that were adorned with three black and white feathers. I laughed out loud. Ralph asked, "What's on your mind?" I looked him in the eyes, smiled, and said, "I'm blessed."

I told Ralph that I was going to look out front and see whether or not Jon and Daniel had returned. He told me that if they have then invite them into the shop. I went to the front of the shop and looking out the windows I could see them in the mustang. They were head banging to some kind of metal music. I unlocked the front door and went out to invite them into Ralph's domain. Daniel looked at me and said, "My boss is pretty cool huh." I replied, "Very cool indeed." Then peering into my eyes Daniel said, "You've had a shot of Spirit Quest haven't you." Smiling I asked, "How do you know?" Of course I knew that Daniel being of Native descent had that special insight into these matters. He looked at me returning my smile and said, "A brother knows these things." It felt good to have someone refer to me as brother.

We all walked into the butcher shop and Ralph said, "I hope you boys are hungry." I'm firing up the grill and we are going to feast on this new side of beef that was freshly killed this morning. He told us to make ourselves at home. We sat at the table in the back and helped ourselves to the plentiful supply of ice cold beer that Ralph had stocked in the fridge. Busy sharpening his instruments, Ralph hollered out, "Drink all you want. If we have to we can raid my stock in the store front." We raised our cans in proper toasting fashion and exclaimed, "To Ralph!" As we touched the cans together and began to guzzle a bit, Ralph started making his professional cuts of beef. It was very interesting to me to actually see the side of beef just 10 feet from me hanging like a food blessing. I thought of how distant we modern humans have become from the food we eat. We no longer look at the animal as a blessed offering who sacrifices their existence to extend our own. Perhaps that is the problem that has created the obesity rates in America. The fact that food has lost the ritualistic spiritual value that should be viewed as an absolutely divine blessing. Delving deeper into my analytical mind I realize that I must shake off my efforts at such philosophical debates and focus on the fun at hand. Daniel looks at me with his insight into my mind and states, "Mr. over Analytical, you better snap out of it." I shook my head and agreed.

Daniel reached into one of the cabinets and pulled out a domino case. He dumped them on the table and inquired, "Who wants to play some bones?" We were all into it. As Daniel swirled the dominos on the table Ralph slapped 4 huge steaks on his gas grill. The steaks hit the hot surface with a sizzle and smell that brought my senses to full alert.

"What's with the absence of traffic on Main St. today?" I Asked Jon. He reminded me that it was Sunday and that most everyone was sitting in church right now. I said, "Oh yeah, I forgot." Daniel said, "Hallelujah, pass the hot sauce." Jon told me not to forget that it was Labor Day weekend and that everyone is off tomorrow so we can enjoy our Sunday in full force. I said, "In that case let me get us all another round of beer."

Daniel told me that he had found out that a bunch of old friends were going to make their way to Sitting Bull Falls in an effort to celebrate the finalization of summer. I thought of how great that would be. I missed that old stomping ground and grew very excited at the opportunity to revisit it. At this point in our conversation Ralph served up our steaks and we began to dig into them. I couldn't help but notice that he had wrapped something up in tin foil and placed it on the grill. I asked Ralph what it was and he told me it was a special cut for his three young friends. He said that he was grill roasting a beef heart for us and that it would serve our minds and bodies well especially in the adventurous atmosphere of Sitting Bull Falls.

Just as we were finishing our steaks and resuming our game of dominos, my senses lit up. My spirit guide came to the forefront of my sight. I could smell the blood dripping from the foil wrapped beef heart as it dropped and sizzled in the fire. Every piece of produce from the front of the store made an interesting collage of smells that drifted into my nose. As my heart rate began to increase and my spirit guide made continual intense glares to the store front, I knew that something very interesting was about to go down.

We heard bells of the front door ring. Ralph looked at Daniel and said, "I guess we forgot to lock the front door." Daniel said it was probably just a customer who didn't read the closed sign. He got up to investigate. I told him to let me lead. We made our way from the rear of the store around the meat counter and up the middle grocery aisle. Just as we were approaching the checkout counters someone in a ski mask came around the end cap of the aisle with a shot gun. The intruder pointed the gun at us and frantically said, "Where's the money?" I was pumped and ready to tango with this son of a bitch. My senses were on extremely high alert and I could smell the desperation and fear in our Assailant. I told the intruder to follow me to the registers and I would give him all the money we had. I could tell that my cooperation put the enemy at little more ease. As I approached the checkout counter I could see in my heightened peripheral vision that the Assailant had dropped his guard and lowered the shot gun. Without hesitation I spun around with a kick that sent the gun flying from his hands straight into the hands of Daniel. Comically I looked at Daniel and said, "Nice catch bro." Daniel seemed a little bewildered at the whole incident. The enemy seemed just as shocked as he just stood there looking at his empty hands. I thought what an idiot as I landed a crushing right hook to his jaw that dropped him like a 150 pound sack of shit. Even though I knew he was out cold I couldn't help but drop a kick into his side that I was sure he would feel for weeks.

By this time Ralph and Jon had made their way to the front of the store. We told them what had just happened and Ralph suggested that we call the cops. I asked him to hold off on that for a while. I stated that we needed to teach this guy a lesson. With my senses still on high alert I could smell the meth creeping out of the enemy's pores. I told my friends that I was well aware of the meth epidemic that was crippling folks here and that the message we would send would be one for every demonic soul in the area. We would send a notice that this place off limits. I looked at Ralph and told him how much gratitude I had for our new found friendship and in an effort to express that gratitude I would like him to allow me to send that message for him. I could tell he was completely on board as he grabbed the attacker by the feet and said, "Help me take him to the back."

We carried the dumb criminal back to our meat hanging dining area and dropped him on the cold hard floor. I asked for some rope and tied his hands together. We lifted him and hung him by his bound hands on a beef hook. I took some water and splashed it in his face. Slowly the idiot began to come around. He started kicking about and yelling. I circled him with some duct tape and bound his legs together. The captive was still trying to shake himself loose as he begged for us to let him go. I looked him in the eyes and said, "I don't have ears to hear your moronic pleas." Then I wrapped duct tape around his mouth and head. Circling the fool, I told him that it took either an extremely brave or stupid man to think that he could come into my friend's establishment waiving a gun around demanding money. With that statement I emphasized my disgust with a punch to the kidneys. The hanging dumbass was making whimpering pleas under the duct tape. I circled him one more time and came to face him. I told him to tell all his cranked out buddies that if any of them so much as looks at this place they will find themselves in a much worse predicament than you. I yelled, "Agreed!" The foe nodded in agreement while still whimpering. I looked at him and stated, "Don't worry it's not over yet. Daniel hand me that two by four." Daniel handed the board to me. I looked at the meth head one last time in the eyes and said, "I have no sympathy for you."

I landed five blows to the body, one to each knee, and a final one to his head that sent him back into unconsciousness.

My new friend Ralph as well as Daniel and Jon, stood in silent awe for a few minutes. Jon said, "Damn Tristan, you've changed a little. I like the new vigilante you. That was like watching something straight out of a crime novel." I laughed and said, "I'm blessed."

We untied the unconscious bastard and took him out front. Ralph made the call to the authorities that quickly made their way to the market. We all explained to the officers how the intruder interrupted our steak lunch and how we made quick work at containing the situation until the authorities arrived. I explained that the assailant might need some medical attention. An ambulance and two officers made their departure to the hospital. The two remaining officers were old high school acquaintances and were invited by Ralph to stay and have a fresh steak. They agreed and we all began to relax and resume our Sunday lunch.

One of the officers was Daniel's cousin and I remembered him well. His name was Chris. Chris told me that he had heard the story of my grandfather's tragic death and gave his condolences. I got the feeling after talking with him for a while that he was insinuating how he wouldn't blame anyone who took a retribution stand against the two idiots that committed the murder. In talking further with Officer Chris, I could sense that he knew how I felt. Without saying it he knew exactly what my intensions were and he fed me with some very useful information. He stated that his other cousin worked as a corrections officer for Western New Mexico Correctional Facility in Grants New Mexico. He went on to inform me that is where the two evil bastards are being detained. Officer Chris then explained to me that they were being transferred to Lea County Correctional facility in Hobbs. He looked at me and asked, "Do you know what that means?" I replied with a look of great satisfaction, "They will probably be taking a route right through here onto Loco Hills to reach Hobbs." Chris nodded yes. I asked him if he knew exactly when this was going to take place. He told me to hang on while he made a phone call.

By now Ralph had already pulled some more fresh steaks off the grill, Daniel and Jon had resumed their game of dominos, and I was elated at my new information. Chris soon returned from using the phone and reported to me that the prison van containing my next prey would be making its way through Artesia on Tuesday. I looked at him and bluntly asked, "What is it going to take to pull off a van jacking without any harm to the correctional officers?" He looked at me with a smile and said, "I thought you might ask that." He explained to me that for the right price anything could be possible. Chris told me that if I could manage to get $50,000 to him by Tuesday morning then he would be able to contact the escorts and explain to them further details pertaining to my plan. He looked at me and asked, "You do have a plan, don't you?" I looked at him and laughed saying, "You'd be surprised at how quickly a plan can come together on a whim." I told him that he would have his money by Tuesday morning and by that night I would have my revenge.

The officers finished their meal, shook all of our hands, and left. Daniel asked me, "How are you planning to come up with $50,000?" I shrugged my shoulders and said, "I haven't got a clue but for now I plan on having a wonderful day with you guys." Chuckling at the thought I said, "Perhaps after finishing my bottle of Spirit Quest tonight I'll have a vision." Ralph said, "Either that or die. Be careful with that stuff. Like I said I have not seen anyone who could finish a pint." I replied, "Bare in mind that if there is a drop of sweat of Grandpa's in this bottle, it shall surely find a way to intermingle with our blood relation and aid me in a higher tolerance." Daniel looked at me and said, "Could you say that in English please?" I laughed and said, "Simply stated, I am blessed."

Chapter 8

Sitting Bull Falls

After finishing up the absolutely wonderfully fresh steak lunch, I thanked Ralph for his generous hospitality. Daniel, Jon, and I began to walk to the front of the butcher shop. Ralph said, "Don't forget your roasted beef heart." I grabbed the paper sack he had put the foil wrapped heart in and headed out the front door. While walking to Jon's mustang, I asked, "Where are we headed now?" Jon said, "How about continuing our fun filled Labor Day weekend in the beautiful atmosphere of Sitting Bull Falls?" I asked, "Did ya'll find out if anyone else we know is going to be there?" Jon looked at Daniel with his ornery smile and said, "Just a few." I looked at them both and said, "What the hell was that funny look for?" Daniel said, "It's a surprise." With that being said I figured we were in for a very eventful Sunday.

We piled into the mustang and headed south on U.S. Highway 285. This route leads to Carlsbad but about halfway between here and there is the turn on State Highway 137 heading South,

South West. We find ourselves in this location making our way toward the Guadalupe Mountains. As we sing, laugh, and sip on a little more beer, the land starts giving way to a spectacular intermingling of plant and animal life. The earth's surface seems to start rolling higher and more complex with rock formations and an occasional small cave makes its opening appearance as to invite any who dare to explore. The air flowing through the mustang is crisp and cleansed by the summer sun. I lay my head back on the seat and thank God for such a beautiful day.

Jon made one final turn into the parking spaces for those who wish to explore the area. There were a few other cars here too and one motorcycle. I wondered what interesting strangers we might encounter and hoped that this wasn't an occasion to kick some ass. Jon grabbed the ice chest. Daniel grabbed the sack with the beef heart. I grabbed a glimpse of my on looking spirit guide and noticed that he seemed happy. I thought, I'll be damned, did he actually just smile. My guide seemed to be enjoying being here in this enchanting atmosphere. I felt more at ease to the fact that this was going to be nothing but a serene pleasure adventure.

The state had laid out a concrete path complete with railing to aid in a hike to the bottom of the water fall. This was always where we went first to see how many tourist or strangers were around. Other times we would hike and climb around to the top of the falls which is usually where the more interesting events took place. Upon reaching the pool area of the waterfall I finally saw the surprise that Jon and Daniel were talking about. Down further on a rock edge where the falling water met the pool was my first childhood love Lisa. I could not believe my eyes. The mist from the water pounding itself created a rainbow of colors that seemed to accentuate her presence. She obviously had been swimming as she was soaked. She had a white T-shirt that covered her underlying red bikini. As she stood there in the swirling mist of colors seemingly in slow motion, she raised both of hands to pull her long brown hair back in order to secure it with a hair band. I was totally mesmerized at the whole spectacle. I looked at Jon and Daniel who were just standing there laughing at my trance like condition. Daniel said, "Close your mouth dude and stop drooling." I replied, "You guys could have warned me." Jon said laughing, "The look on your face just now is well worth the deception."

In her company were three other wonderful childhood female friends, Delsa, Joy, and Liz. All four of them came running up to great us with hugs and smiles. We all started talking and reminiscing. Finally I got the chance to pull Lisa aside and talk with her in a more private location. She asked, "So how have you been?" I told her of my recent journeys but spared her any violent details. We spoke of how we first had eyes for each other and how the purity of that first taste of love would be forever engrained in that 8th grade year. She finally laid that inevitable question on me that I had no answer for back then, "Why did you break up with me?" I told her that I had a lot of time to ponder that same question. Pride got in my way back then and I didn't have the humble sensibilities that I now possess or the communication skills. I told her that it was totally out of self loathing. After meeting her dad one day I soon realized that I was completely outclassed. I went on to say that I had never had the pleasure of being around such successful people who were obviously well educated. Her dad being a doctor and me being trailer park trash made me feel as if I could never fit into her life as the person she deserved. I took her by the hands, looked her in the eyes and said, "As much as it hurt both of us, I knew it was the right thing to do." I told her that I still didn't have my shit together and look at how far she had come. We agreed to leave everything in the past and to remain just friends. As she hugged me, the comfort of closure warmed my heart and even brought out a tear.

The ladies who once were our partners in crime as teenage rebels still held us captivated at their beauty and ability to party with the best of us. They said that they were going to head back to town to get ready for the gravel pit party tonight. We all hugged and promised to be there. The ladies left and we commenced to being the crazy young men that we are.

We were climbing the surrounding rock formations and doing cannon ball jumps and suicidal dives into the water. As we finally started to wear ourselves out a little, we gathered on one big sun drenched rock about the size of a bus and began to talk. We kept cracking open the beer but with all of the exercise and fun, the cool refreshing beverage had no affect on us. I asked Daniel where the food was and he ran down to get the sack that was behind a bush. He made his way back to the top of the huge rock, sat next to us, and opened up the sack. Looking and reaching inside he said, "Oh cool, Ralph put some of his home made tortillas and hot sauce in here to go with the beef heart." We quickly tore into the meat, ripping it with our hands and lining up our burritos. Daniel said, "Right on, he packed us two hearts." He looked at me and Jon and asked, "Have either of you had beef heart?" Unable to speak because of our extremely full mouths Jon and I shook our heads no. Daniel told us that he had eaten it before and it seemed to give him strange dreams. He said that the night after consuming several beef heart burritos that he fell asleep and started dreaming about the ocean. He said that he had two dolphins strapped on his feet like water skies. He had them harnessed in a fashion that allowed him to ride them as such. He said it was a wonderful dream and that he wondered if it had anything to do with eating the heart of an animal. I said, "It might have aided you in finding your animal guide." He agreed and we devoured the rest of our meal.

Feeling rejuvenated, we decided to explore the top area of the falls. We hiked our way to the point where the water takes it first leap over the edge. Looking at my friends and beautiful surroundings I couldn't help but stretch out my arms and say aloud, "Thank you!" Jon and Daniel looked at me and asked, "Who are you talking to?" I said, "My maker of course." Jon looked at me and said, "That's what I've always liked about you Tristan, you always dance to the beat of your own drum." I thanked Jon for his compliment and we started to explore up stream. As we made our way over rocks, around bushes, and through the upstream paths, Daniel asked, "Do you guys remember that chemically enhanced night we spent up here?" I replied, "Regretfully, I remember all of that night. Thank God we don't get stupid like that anymore."

After about a mile of hiking further into the Guadalupe Mountains we came across a camp site. As we made our approach to investigate, a stocky older Man of about 50 came marching toward us. With my guard up I introduced myself and reached out a hand to shake. Luckily the man seemed to be friendly and took my hand and said his name was Monty. He was a strongly built man, not tall but had shoulders about as wide as his height. You could tell at a glance that his arms could become pythons and squeeze the life out of any who dare to engage in a physical bout. His shoulder length hair was turning grey as was his well established mustache and beard. He had several tattoos and wore a leather vest with obvious motorcycle affiliation colors adorning it. I said, "That must be your bike we saw in the parking lot." He said that it was and asked us to sit and join him as he was brewing up some tea. We did as he suggested and he began to tell us about his journey. He said that he was exploring America on motorcycle. Monty told us that he would travel coast to coast stopping only now and then to check in with a nationwide temp service to get enough work to provide for a few weeks of fun and adventure then back on the road he would go. "Now that sounds like freedom and fun," Daniel said. "Indeed it is my new friend," Monty said.

Monty had a percolating campfire coffee pot that was beginning to steam. He said that he only had one cup but that we could pass the tea around if we liked. I asked him, "What cha got in that tea?" With a smile Monty replied, "Just some secret herbs I rounded up here. It will cure what ails you." We each take our turn at sipping some of the unknown substance and agreed that we should be getting back. We all shook biker Monty's hand and returned back from the way we came.

As we were just about to reach the top of the falling water, I started chuckling a little. Jon and Daniel started in with laughter as well. Before we could do anything else we had to sit on the same huge rock we ate on and laugh. We were holding our stomachs from the uncontrollable bellowing laughter that filled our spirits. After about 10 minutes of feeling absolutely elated we regained our senses and resumed our trek toward Jon's car. Before we entered the mustang we leaned on it in subtle reflection as Daniel said, "That was one hell of a good sip of tea." Laughing even more I replied, "Man I know. I hope that I can survive the night. I have had beef heart, mystery tea, and tonight I'm gonna make my attempt at finishing my bottle of Spirit Quest." Jon looked at me while shaking his head, smiling, and said, "Good luck with that Bro."

We loaded into the mustang, cranked on the music, and returned to Daniels house. I thanked Jon for the wonderful cruise, shook his hand, and we shared one of our manly friendship hugs. I asked him if he was going to make it to the gravel pit party and he just said, "I'm not sure. I'll see ya when I see ya." With that Jon got into his mustang, turned up the music, and made a peeling out departure. I stood there waiving to his tail lights and stated, "Until we meet again my good friend, farewell."

Chapter 9

Pecos River

Daniel and I decided to take a shower and prepare ourselves for the continuation of our Labor Day weekend fun. After making ourselves presentable by sight and smell I looked at Daniel and said, "We sure clean up nice, huh." He laughed and said, "I don't know about you but I sure do." With that comment being said we had to rough house a little. I said, "It's a good thing we both decided to finally get rid of our 80's hair or we would be in the mirror trying to fix it." Daniel laughed and said, "What were we thinking back then?" I said, "I think it was our individuality that ached to show the world that we don't all fit into its cookie cutter ideas." "Oh yeah," said Daniel.

Daniel asked if we were going to take my caddy or his pickup. I told him that I needed to conserve what little gas I had to finish out my tasks. Daniel told me that he knew of a way for me to make some quick money. "Do tell." I said. He told me that this Labor Day weekend Sunday night had been scheduled for an open night in the underground realm of extreme fighting. He said that this sort of thing has been gaining in popularity over the past couple of years. He said that he knew a guy who could set up a quick battle for me. The winner takes all of $500. The loser gets nothing. "Of course, the side bets are where all the money is being thrown about," Daniel said. I asked him where we needed to be and when. He told me to hold my horses while he made a quick phone call.

My adrenaline was starting to build at the thought of battling for cash. This would be something entirely new for me. I wondered how good I could fight without having a justified reason other than for money. I could certainly use $500 and relaxed with that thought as the justification I needed.

Daniel returned from being on the phone. He told me that we had been booked for an early fight at 8:00 p.m. at the Pecos River crossing just east of the trailer park I grew up in. I looked at my watch and saw that it was 6:00 p.m. I told Daniel that gave us enough time to visit my old home, show up and beat some ass for money, and then make our way to the gravel pit party. Daniel smiled and said, "Sounds like a plan." We jumped into his pickup and headed to the run down trailer park I once called home.

Approaching the dilapidated trailer park on the north side of Artesia, I couldn't help but allow hatred fill my heart. I kept remembering all the things that have led me back here to carry out some much deserved retribution. I told Daniel that this was exactly what I needed to fuel my aggression before the fight. As we made our way toward the back of the park to the location of my childhood home, I thought to myself, how depressingly ugly everything here is. Strolling down this memory lane of abandoned trailers and poverty, I couldn't help but see the similarities of the spectacle and the ugly rage that has consumed me for so long.

We finally came to the actual trailer that I grew up in and stopped. It was abandoned and overgrown with the trees I remembered planting as a child. I got out of the pickup and began to approach the place. With every step I blocked out a haunting memory. Finally approaching the front door, I took a deep breath, and opened it. As I walked inside I couldn't help but feel like a giant. As a child I guess everything was bigger by comparison. Now that I have physically grown, everything seems out of proportion to my memories. I laughed to myself and thought I am bigger than my haunting memories and walked through the house feeling 10 feet tall and able to squash anything in my path. Feeling more at ease with my return home I look at Daniel and say, "Let's go win some money!" We jumped back into his pickup and headed to the Pecos River.

The pavement finally gave way to dirt road and after crossing several cattle guards I could see the line of trees and growth that followed the river. The sandy road led right into a river crossing that was paved. The crossing had about 6 inches of water flowing over it. I remembered as a kid always feeling excited at the possibility of being swept away by the current. We crossed the river with no problems and drove up the embankment on the other side. The land gave way to a level clearing that was outlined in a circle by vehicles and people. A fight was obviously well under way as the crowd was cheering in great blood thirsty fashion.

Daniel parked the pickup and we made our way to the crowd. As we approached the dramatic scene of barbaric proportions, I could see two men about my age who were trading punches and seemed to be very tired. The spectators were yelling for more action while holding fists of money. Finally one of the fighters landed a crushing blow to his opponent that knocked him out. The congregation of thrill seekers let out a final unified burst of exclamation then commenced to settling bets.

Daniel motioned me over to a man he had been talking with. I went over to them and soon realized who the man was, Chente. He was obviously Native American well versed in Spanish and English. He was another childhood friend. Chente, a smaller man, seemed to be the ring leader of the whole event. I could tell by his surrounding entourage that he was a man to be respected in this atmosphere. Chente looked at me, shook my hand, and said, "One rule, no rules." He then went about his business of counting money. I looked at Daniel and said, "Come on man there has to be some kind of order in these fights." Daniel replied, "Either the loser passes out or tries real hard to act like he did. Otherwise the fight could go on forever. There are no tap outs." I asked Daniel, "Has any been killed doing this?" His reply was, "Not recently." "That's comforting," I said sarcastically. I asked Daniel who I would be fighting and hoped it was someone I could learn to hate real fast. He told me that it was one of the "Roid Brothers". Cool, I thought, it was someone for which I already had a great deal of disgust.

As a young teenager they were two older guys in their twenties that would show up at our high school parties looking to cause trouble. They were notorious for using steroids. Hence the name we gave them the "Roid Brothers." It really didn't matter to me which one I would have the pleasure of beating. I just had to keep an eye out for the other because of their inseparable bond. I remembered the both of them terrorizing the younger, much smaller kids back in the day. I had seen them gang up on victims and damn near beat them to death in a fit of senseless roid rage.

Daniel told me that it was time to enter the fighting area. I felt a little nervous but realized that it was a good thing that my adrenaline was pumping somewhat. I figured that I should put on my game face and started pacing the arena with a look of intensity. My opponent had yet to appear from the crowd. I searched the surrounding mob for my spirit guide and saw him sitting on top of Daniels pickup. He looked as if he was just one of the spectators with no real concern about the matter. I kind of laughed to myself and sarcastically thought, thanks for the support. Finally a huge man made his appearance to the chanting calls of the people. They were chanting over and over, "Evil." I looked at Daniel and said, "So Evil does have a face." He laughed and said, "Good luck Bro."

I couldn't help but think that this son of a bitch must have been doing steroids his entire life because he was one of the most muscle bound bastards I have ever seen in person. It seemed unreal, the deformed figure that looked at me as if I were to be his next meal. He was accompanied to the sandy fighting ring by his brother. The only thing I recognized was their faces because they seemed to have tripled in size. I thought, oh great, I know Evil's brother isn't going to like the fact that I'm about to kick his sibling's ass. I had to smile at my great optimism.

Chente made the indication of action by leaning over and swinging his arm down. With that setting our fate in motion, the crowd began to call out with blood lust and Evil made his way swiftly to where I stood. As if the earth was mocking me, I slipped on a rock and fell to one knee. My opponent made quick work of his advantage as he wrapped me up from behind and before I could even blink he had me over his head and threw me into the assembled onlookers. I immediately made my way to my feet. Evil mistakenly had his back turned to me as he had his arms raised to provoke the crowd into another chant of his name. I took full advantage of this and jumped with both feet landing at an angle on his right knee. I could feel the crumbling of his lower leg and sensed the complete snap of his knee joint. As my adversary winced in pain and fell to his other knee, I quickly grabbed his head with both of my hands and crushed my right knee into his face. I whispered into his ear as I grabbed his hair with my left hand, "Arrogance serves no one at all." I then started hitting him in the face repeatedly until I could see that he was without a doubt unconscious. I quickly scanned the area, looking for his brother to avenge him. Sure enough the knocked out muscle man's Roid Brother was starting to make an aggressive approach when Chente stepped up and pointed a gun in his face. Chente's obvious supporting cast followed in the same fashion with their guns. Chente said to him, "If you want to fight here, you have to schedule, agreed?" Roid brother replied, "Agreed." Roid Brother picked his sibling up and made his way out of the arena. The crowd that had been hushed at the whole gun pointing incident slowly began to chant a new name, Tristan. I smiled and received my $500 from Chente. He shook my hand and pulled me in to hug my neck and said, "It's been too long my friend." I replied,

"Too long indeed." Without missing a beat Chente resumed his betting activities and Daniel and I returned to his pickup.

As I jumped into the pickup and began counting my money, Daniel hopped into the driver's side with an enthusiastic, "Hell yeah!" I was just smiling from ear to ear and even started to laugh a little. Daniel asked, "Whatcha thinkin?" I looked at him and stated with a smile, "I'm blessed." Daniel replied, "I'm beginning to realize that."

Daniel asked me if I had given anymore thought to the $50,000 deal brought up by Officer Chris. I told him that I was sure that tonight's gravel pit party would serve me well with the insight needed to make a clear or perhaps not so clear decision on the matter. I told Daniel while being optimistic; I still had until Tuesday morning to come up with the money and a plan. "For now," I said, "I think I'll have a shot of Spirit Quest to start my celebration, search, and memorial." Daniel asked, "Do you think you can finish the bottle." I replied, "I know I'll finish it. Whether I survive or not that is the question." With a huge smile, I reached under the seat, pulled out my bottle and took a guzzling swig that brought the remaining level to half way. Daniel said, "Don't worry man; I'll keep an eye on you." I replied, "You're a good friend Bro."

We made our way back to town and then a little south to an area where the ground opened up into several giant pits. Each pit had either gravel, caliche dirt, or some other earthly mounds of interest. Daniel pulled to the edge of the gravel pit that opened up deep into the earth's surface. The sun was setting and sending up the last of its gloriously colored rays. The planners of this party were well prepared with a pile of wood that would make any pyromaniac drool with excitement. A fire of the size of a small car had already been lit and was sending up flames as to mock the dying sun. Several vehicles made a large circle around the bon fire. People where well into socializing while making frequent trips to the iced down keg. Staring at the event I stated with a sarcastically dramatic soft voice, "What a magnificent sight." Daniel following my lead held a hand over his heart and said, "If this is heaven, let me die now." We started laughing and he pulled the pickup down into the pit to join everyone else.

We made our social rounds, shaking hands, giving hugs, and sharing what's new. After letting everyone know that we had arrived, I pulled Daniel to the side and said, "Looks like this is going to be a very serene and calm party. I think I'm gonna head up the other side of the pit and watch from above while I sip on my bottle and reflect on my situation." Daniel said, "All right Bro, if you need me I'm here for you."

I headed away from the glow of the fire and up the side of the pit that was more dirt that gravel. I made my way to the top edge of the pit and took a seat on an old tractor tire. I could vaguely hear voices coming from the party and the occasional burst of laughter. I took another sip of Grandpa's special elixir and felt the burning sensation down my throat and into my brain. I could not stand the anticipation of finishing the bottle any longer so with one last upturn I swigged the remaining hooch. While watching the crowd down below, the fire seemed to rise higher and higher. The colors from the flames were no longer the traditional red and yellow but swirled with vibrant purples and pinks. The smoke that rose was making animal formations that would disappear then reappear as something different. My spirit guide was chanting, dancing around the fire, and through the surrounding people. My mind started to fill with images from my childhood, my recent past, and scenes that have not taken place yet. Every violent encounter to this point flashed in my mind. The beat of an unseen drum increased with every clip of thought. My guide was speeding up with chants and foot pounding dance rhythm. My heart was beating so hard that I could see and feel my whole body bouncing. All of the sudden the beating of the drum stopped and everything fell silent. Looking at the party below it seemed if everything froze and time came to a halt. My mind started to escape my body and I began to float. I looked down from above and could see my body laying asleep and looking peaceful. The smoke from the fire was the only motion that came from the paused party scene. The pink and purple smoke swirled higher and toward me. It seemed to wrap around my waist and pull me through the night air into the west direction. As I fly through the twilight I can see the area below. I saw the small town of Hope and the only church there. I saw the hills start rolling into mountains. My spirit still being pulled through the night air by the mystical smoke, made its way to the edge of the Sacramento Mountains. The smoking guidance stopped its pulling and allowed me to view the area below for awhile. I could see a sign that read, "Woe, you passed Mayhill." I remembered this place from my childhood. All of the sudden a full grown black bear made his appearance. The bear stood up looked at me and fell back in unrestrained laughter. He began to roll around chuckling then seemed to regain his composure and walked back into the woods. I could not help but laugh myself. I thought, how strange to see a laughing bear. Just then the smoke jerked my floating self back to the eastern direction. My spirit drifted swiftly back to the gravel pits and I could see Daniel kneeling beside my body. He was shaking me and yelling my name. My spirit quickly reentered my body and my eyes opened. I looked at Daniel and said with a smile, "Just having a little spirit quest Bro." He said, "Don't you do that again asshole!" "Do what?" I asked. "Scare me like that." I told Daniel that I was sorry but I did have an interesting vision. I told him what I saw and knew that the next morning I would have to depart to Mayhill. I said, "But for now, party on!" I sprung to my feet and headed for the keg. Daniel said while walking behind me, "You are one crazy dude."

Chapter 10

Mayhill

The gravel pit party served us well. We caught up will many old friends and even made some new ones. After the party fizzled out, Daniel and I returned to his house. I thanked Daniel for allowing me to crash on his couch. I told him that this would probably be the last time and that in the morning I would be off to Mayhill to see what the vision held in store for me. He told me that he wanted to help. I thanked him for all that he had done and insisted that I finish out my vengeance solo. I explained that the less he knew about my actions and the less he was involved, it would protect him from any prosecution. He reluctantly agreed and we both quickly fell asleep.

I was awakened at the crack of dawn by a very enthusiastic rooster that cried his alarm from outside the house. Without disturbing my friend, I made my way out to the Caddy. I hopped in and started it up. I looked at the fuel gauge that read almost empty. I remembered the fight prize money that I still had in my wallet and made my way to a gas station on the western edge of tiny Artesia. I walked inside the small convenience store to pay for some gas and asked the clerk if I could fill it up. The clerk agreed and I returned to the fuel pumps. As I removed the gas cap and inserted the nozzle, I saw an older man riding a bicycle down Main Street. I could not believe my eyes. It was Whistling Benny.

Whistling Benny is a shell shocked man that has a few mental issues. He is of average height and slender build. There wasn't an ounce of fat on him probably from the constant bike riding. Although he doesn't seem to have very much muscle, I had heard stories as a kid that he possesses the strength of at least two men. He got the name Whistling Benny from his notorious hatred of people who whistled. My mom explained to me that any whistling sound probably brought back memories of falling shells in the war. I remembered some of the kids, when I was a child, would whistle at him when they saw him. He has a remarkable ability to ride his bicycle, locate a rock on the ground, and without stopping his bike he could take one foot and kick the rock straight as a bullet toward any who dared mock him. Another memory I had of him was again as a small child, downtown on Main Street, Whistling Benny was stopping all the traffic in both directions trying to figure out who was whistling. The whistling was coming from a painter on the second floor landing of a building. The painter was totally oblivious to what was going on below. Now here he is as I fuel my car approaching me with great speed. He came to an abrupt stop about ten feet from me. He got off of his bicycle and came straight to me. I thought, oh Lord, what now. Benny stood in front of me in a very uncomfortable distance of about one foot. I politely asked him, "Can I help you?" I could not help but notice the contrast of his old leather face that had the youngest most vibrant blue eyes imaginable. He just looked me over for a few seconds and said with a straight face, "Don't worry, you will find it." I asked him, "Find what?" At that point he mounted his bicycle again and departed while mumbling over and over, "You will find it."

My tank was now full and I went back inside the store to pay for the gas. The middle aged male clerk took my money and told me, "That was strange." I asked him, "What do you mean?" The clerk told me that Whistling Benny had been on his death bed for about a month and that no one expected him to make it much longer. I replied, "That was strange indeed."

I made my way back to my Caddy, entered, and began to drive due west toward the Sacramento Mountains. The fresh morning summer air made its way through my opened windows. I heard an eagle cry and saw the majestic bird swoop down in a northern direction which brought my attention to Whistling Benny who was standing next to his bike waving as if to bid me farewell. As I drove by I could still hear him mumbling, "You will find it."

With Benny and Artesia in my rearview mirror, I hit the accelerator and laid down some tread. I reached for a smoke and started to realize how close I am to my window of opportunity with the imprisoned assholes. I think, ok, today is Monday and Officer Chris told me that the $50,000 payment for cooperation had to be in by Tuesday morning. I laughed at my situation and thought, and here I am chasing my vision into the mountains with less than $500 dollars and one day to come up with the rest. I could see my spirit guide galloping on his horse as if to keep up with me and I smiled while once again proclaiming out loud, "I am blessed."

About 20 miles heading west from Artesia I slowed down to enter the even smaller town of Hope. Hope, New Mexico has one post office, a few old buildings not being used, and one small church that I know of. The same church that I hear dear old dad has been attending and providing his hypocritical leadership. This place reminds me of the old west movies where there was just one street with a handful of buildings that served at a meeting place of commerce for the surrounding rural community. The only thing it lacked was a saloon.

I drove slowly through the area and reached the western side of the tiny town. I could see to the north the cemetery where several of my relatives from my dad's side lay to rest. There were a thousand controversial thoughts that were swirling through my head. I had to shake off the ensuing events that would follow my current task at hand.

The tiny two lane highway that I'm on starts to conform to the land as the rolling foot hills begin to mature into the majesty of the Sacramento Mountains. After a few more miles of absorbing the beauty that surrounds this area, I made my approach to the small mountain town of Mayhill. This place was about the size of the town of Hope but buzzed with a lot more life. On one side of the small strip there was the post office and a restaurant. On the other side there was a hardware store and a Bar.

I was extremely hungry at this point and hoped that the restaurant was open. I parked my car on the sloping edge of the building. It was kind of cool to be parking next to horses that had been tied to the wooden rail which ran in front of the building. I was glad to see that the restaurant was open this early and it smelled like the grill was in full operation. I remembered stopping here as a kid and listening to my mom remark on how this restaurant had the best Mexican food in all of New Mexico. I hoped that it was still true.

Looking at my watch I could see that it was 10:30 and hoped that they were serving lunch. I stepped up onto the wooden deck that lined the front of both the restaurant and the post office. I opened the door to the restaurant and entered to see that I was the only customer. A native woman with a Spanish accent came from the back with enthusiasm. She had a gleaming smile and grabbed the pencil from behind her ear in a prompt manner to take my order. She asked, "What to drink?" I said, "I'll have iced tea please." She said that she would be right back as she handed me a menu.

I hadn't chosen a table yet and opted for one that overlooked the front windows and door. Off in a corner chair I could see my car, the road out front, and the bar across the street. I felt comfortable and starved as the waitress returned. She set my tea and some corn chips with salsa down and asked, "What to eat?" I asked her if they still served stacked enchiladas. She said, "Si." I then told her that I wanted the biggest stack of green chili enchiladas that they could fit on a plate and to top it off with three fried eggs. I asked if it came with beans and rice. Again she replied, "Si." She swiftly returned to the kitchen.

I began to munch on the chips and hot sauce like a man who had just came out of the woods with nothing to eat for days. By the time I finished all the chips the waitress returned with my order and another basket of chips. I thought what a beautiful spread. I quickly devoured the meal while thinking how right my mom was in her declaration that this is the best Mexican food place in all of New Mexico.

There were ash trays on the tables so I assumed it was safe to light up and did. As I sat there relaxed and satisfied with my wonderful meal, the waitress sat at a table on the other side and had a smoke as well. I snuffed my butt, got up, and went over to her table. She looked up and asked if I needed anything else. I told her that I needed some information. She told me to sit and ask away. I told her that my story might sound a little crazy but that I had a vision that led me here. She didn't even blink an eye and said, "I'm with you so far." I told her that in my vision I saw a laughing bear and asked her if that meant anything to her. With a smile she said that it might mean something but the man I need to speak with was tending bar across the street. I thanked her for her hospitality, paid for the meal, left a sizeable tip, and stepped outside.

I began to cross the street as rain started falling in drops so big that just one could wet your entire head. I jumped under the porch in front of the bar and shook myself off a bit. Thunder began to roar so loud that I knew I had better get inside fast. I wondered if my guide was still around. To my surprise as I opened the bar door, my guide had already found a dry comfortable table off in the corner. I could not help but laugh a little at his uncharacteristic need for shelter. The only person in the place was the bar tender. He was listening to a rock and roll station on the radio while cleaning glasses. The man seemed to be about 45 with long straight black hair that was starting to grey. He was dressed in all black and had a huge hunting knife in its sheath connected to his belt and strapped to his leg. He had a mustache and goatee that shared the same salt and pepper as his hair. He looked up from his work and greeted me by saying, "Come on in. What will it be?" I went to the far end of the bar that bent around in order to provided whoever sat there with a view of the front door. As I sat on the stool and leaned on the bar, I replied, "A beer with a shot of Tequila." He said, "Coming up." As I pondered my situation for a second I quickly said, "On second thought, I'll have a shot of Spirit Quest." The bar tender stopped reaching for the Tequila. He then opened my beer and brought it to me. As he handed me my beer he looked hard as he searched my eyes with his own. After about ten seconds of looking me in the eyes, he scanned the rest of me. He said, "You have the look of your Grandfather. You are in luck. I have been saving my last bottle of Spirit Quest for just such an occasion."

Feeling at ease with the thought of being in the company of someone who shared my interests, I quickly downed the beer and asked for another. The bar tender poured two shots, grabbed one, and said, "To Bruce." I followed with the same. I introduced myself as Tristan and he told me his name was Cloud Dancer. Cloud Dancer said, "I'm sorry for your loss. What is it that brings you here?" I told him of my vision. I told him of the laughing bear. He shook his head as if to understand every unconceivable thing of which I spoke. I could not help but smile at the thought of being in such company. Cloud Dancer asked, "What do you find amusing?" I replied, "I just get exceedingly happy at times when I feel blessed. Right now my blessing lies in the fact that the first two people I have encountered here in the mountains have not looked at me as if I was completely crazy." He replied, "That's because you are amongst kindred spirits. Your Grandfather felt the same way." He went on to tell me that the interpretation of my vision was an easy one for those in the know. Cloud Dancer said that my Grandfather's long trusted Navajo friend is named Laughing Bear. I asked how I could find Laughing Bear. Cloud Dancer asked me what kind of quest I was on. I told him that I am on a vengeance quest. He said, "Well all right then." He told me that if I drove further into the mountains about one mile on the main road that I would see a pasture to the south. On that pasture there would be only one huge Weeping Willow tree. There is a scarcely used dirt road that leads from the main road due south to that tree. The tree would be at the base of the adjoining mountain. From that tree you will have to hike due south over that mountain and two more because there are no roads that lead to Laughing Bears dwelling. I asked him how many hours it would take. He looked me over and said, "For you, about 2 hours as long as your guide over there pushes you along." I said, "So you can see him over there?" "Certainly," he said.

Feeling more and more at ease with my own sanity and the comfortable understanding of the mountain people; I stood with pride, thanked Cloud Dancer, and felt as if I floated to the door. My spirit guide was already mounted up and ready to ride as I quickly made my way to the Caddy. The rain had died down to a slow drizzle. I cranked up the engine and slowly backed onto the main road. Both Cloud Dancer and the waitress were outside on opposite sides of the road. They were smiling and waving to me as I made my departure.

As I made my way west, the air was thick with moisture. I could actually see the surrounding clouds as I drove my car through them. The puffy white sections of air seemed to hover around like islands. The clouds presented themselves as landing pads for my guide while riding his white horse. They would jump from one to the other in seemingly slow motion and full of extreme grace. The entire atmosphere was so surreal that I felt as if anything was possible. The pasture that Cloud Dancer spoke of came into view. It was flowing with waves of green grass and had a few buffalo grazing on it. I turned south and headed to the lone Weeping Willow.

I got out of my car and headed directly to the base of the mountain. With my internal compass feeling the pull of due south I headed up the mountain. The ground was soft and slick with pine needles and proved hard to make a foothold at times but my legs didn't seem to mind as they continually churned at the ground. Up and over the first two mountains I went and stopped at the base of the third and final one. I looked up and took several deep breaths. My body was burning from the exertion. The thought of meeting Laughing Bear quickly repaired my fatigue and my body carried me to the top of the final mountain effortlessly.

Looking down the mountain to the valley below, I could see a beautiful log cabin. The cabin had a rock chimney that was bellowing smoke. I seemed to glide all the way down to the front porch of the dwelling. A voice from inside said, "Come in Tristan." I opened the heavy wooden door and stepped inside.

To the left was the huge rock fire place that was crackling with excitement and provided an interesting glow. The glow lit up the grey haired man that sat in a rocking chair facing the door. The bronze aging skin of his face provided a contrasting background for his eyes that were as grey as his long straight hair. He was smoking a pipe that filled the air with an aroma unlike any I had ever smelled. I said, "You must be Laughing Bear." He nodded yes while taking a drag off of his pipe. I asked, "How did you know who I am?" He replied, "It could be that the wind brought me the information. Or, it could be that contraption over there." He pointed to a telephone on the wall behind me. I busted out laughing and Laughing Bear joined me. We regained our composure and Laughing Bear stood up, came over to me, and gave me a hug. While patting me on the back he said, "You have your Grandfathers laugh." I replied, "You have a good sense of humor." He said, "With a name like Laughing Bear, would you expect anything less?"

Laughing Bear told me to join him by the fire. I took a seat in the rocking chair that faced his. We were separated by a bear skin rug on the floor. He told me to prop my feet on the rock ledge that surrounded the face of the fire place. The heat served me well as my boots were wet from the hike and my clothes were damp from rain and sweat. He said, "Will you join me in a smoke?" I replied, "You bet I will." He pointed to the small table next to my chair. On it was a pipe that had already been packed full. The pipe was about six inches long and was carved out of a single piece of wood. I pulled my lighter from my pocket and quickly lit the pipe. After a few large puffs, I began to relax as Laughing Bear began telling me of my Grandpa's story. He told me how he met my Grandpa in a Cantina down in Juarez, Mexico. They were both young and in there early twenties. Grandpa was working on some entrepreneur adventures to say the least and Laughing Bear was working on a good time with the Senorita who was tending bar. Laughing Bear said, "One thing led to another and come to find out, the same man who was meeting your Grandfather for a business transaction was the same man who was married to the beautiful Senorita I was kissing as he walked into the bar." He said that all hell broke loose and that they were lucky to make it back to the states alive. He said, "From then on we were blood brothers for life."

Laughing Bear asked me what I was seeking. I told him of my vision that led me to him and of my quest to deal with the trash that murdered Grandpa. I told him of my limited time frame and how weird I felt at the moment to be laying this all on him. He told me, "Don't you worry Tristan. There is a reason for your being here." He got up and walked over to one of the log walls. Kneeling down, he hit the bottom log of the wall. The log popped open to reveal that it was a fake and a concealing cover for what lay behind. Laughing Bear pulled out a wooden box about the size of a cigarette pack. He handed it to me and said, "Your grandfather told me that in the event of his death, whoever has the vision to seek out Laughing Bear should receive this box and its contents."

I opened the lid to the box and saw a key that lay on top of a folded piece of notebook paper. The key was attached to a leather strap so I hung it around my neck. I unfolded the paper and began to read. It said, "For the seeker of truth. Key # 55 to a safety deposit box in the National Bank in Artesia." Feeling a sense of comfort couple by further curiosity, I thanked Laughing Bear for everything and told him that I was pressed for time. I told him that I needed to make the two hour hike back over the mountains to my car. Laughing Bear said, "Why didn't you just use the road that cuts through a pass from the bar to the back of my house?" I told him that Cloud Dancer gave me the hiking directions and that he said there were no roads leading to your house. Laughing Bear chuckled and said, "Cloud Dancer is my son and shares the same sense of humor."

Laughing Bear said that he would take me back in his Jeep. He said that it would only take about thirty minutes. The rain had let up but the clouds were still dominating the day. The Jeep was dry inside the adjoining garage. With the soft top off of the Jeep we began our trip back to Mayhill's main street. The path was well hidden and stretched through a pass that led right to the rear of the bar I was in earlier. We came out onto the main road and turned in front of the bar. Cloud Dancer was standing on the porch in front having a beer. He saw us drive past and with a huge grin on his face gave me a congratulating thumb up. I returned his smile and nodded my head in a "you got me" fashion.

We made our way to the pasture and turned toward my Caddy that was now surrounded by three Buffalo. After reaching my vehicle and stopping the Jeep, Laughing Bear turned to me and said, "Good Luck Tristan." I thanked him again and before I could get out of the Jeep one of the Buffalo swiftly made its way to my side. I could not open the door. The animal stuck his head over the door and his nose was inches from my face. The huge Buffalo exhaled a mammoth breath through his nose that landed mucus all over me. Laughing Bear snickered and said,

"That is good luck." I said, "Oh really?" He said, "Either that or the damn thing just has a cold." I laughed and said, "I'll view it as luck." I shook Laughing Bears hand and made my way to the Caddy.

Chapter 11

Loco Hills

With great enthusiasm I drove all the way back to Artesia with what seemed to be lightning speed. Noticing the fuel gauge, I pulled into the small convenience store I had visited earlier. I went in to tell the clerk that I was going to fill up on pump 5. The busy clerk nodded yes without looking up at me. I topped of my tank and went back inside to pay. Now with no other customers in the store the clerk seemed to recognize me. As I handed him the money for gas he handed me a folded note. He said that it was from Whistling Benny who had passed away just after our meeting this morning. I unfolded the note which read, "Congratulations, you found it."

I thanked the clerk and feeling very spiritually surrounded, I glided back to my car and decided I needed a little time to think. It was nearing the early evening hours. Being Labor Day I knew that the banks were closed so I concluded that the best thing to do would be to get a motel room. The first place I saw was the Pecos

Inn on Main Street. I pulled into the parking lot and made my way to the front desk. The clerk behind the desk was an elderly grey haired man who handed me key #5. I could not believe the numeric luck that has been surrounding me on my entire quest. I grabbed the key and headed to room number five.

Entering the room I was starting to feel the anxiety of my quest nearing its climactic end and the room began to spin. I threw myself on the bed and said a little prayer for peace. Just as the room stopped spinning the phone rang. I answered it, "Hello." The voice on the other end said, "We need to talk." I asked, "Who is this?" He said, "Officer Chris." I asked, "How the hell did you know where I was?" He replied, "It's a small town. I'll be there in five minutes."

Officer Chris knocked on the door and I let him in. He asked me if I had come up with a plan. I told him that it all depended on my visit to the bank in the morning. He laughed and said, "What are you going to do. Get a vigilante loan?" I laughed with him and said, "I really don't know what to expect tomorrow." Officer Chris said, "You're not planning on robbing the bank, are you?" I assured him that I was not a thief. I went on to tell him that whatever lawful boundaries I have to cross for true justice should not even be boundaries at all. I assured him that by 9:30 a.m. he should know whether or not I had the $50,000 to cover the expense of allowing me safe capture of my two enemies.

Chris told me that the correctional van would be making its way through Artesia at 11:00 a.m. and that is where the corrections officers are to stop and phone in to him. Chris said that at that time he would let them know what the plan is going to be. I told Chris to meet me back in this hotel room at 9:30 a.m. and we would hash out the details. He agreed and left me to my thoughts.

The one enemy I had surrounding me at this moment was time. I began to pace the floor. I started to think about the brutal death of my Grandpa. Vengeance filled my heart and I could not help but wail into a pillow so that people could not hear me. My eyes began to swell with the tears of hatred and loss. My mind was almost out of control when I fell to the bed in exhaustion. I drifted in a dreamlike but conscience state. I pondered through every instance that brought me to this point. As luck would have it my exhausted drifting gave way to time consumption and before I could blink an eye it was 8:45 a.m.

I shook off the night's memory lane and jumped into my car to head down Main Street. I quickly pulled into the parking lot of the bank which held an answer to my mystery key. Someone was just unlocking the door when I pulled it open and said, "I need to talk to the manager." The young bank clerk asked, "Is there a problem?" I told her that there was no problem but that I urgently needed to match this key to its box. I held up the key that had the number 55 stamped on it. She said, "We have been expecting you Tristan." I asked her how she knew my name. She told me that my Grandpa was a very special customer and that he said his grandson Tristan might show up in urgent manner to claim what is his. She told me to follow her to the safety deposit box vault. She asked for the key and I handed it to her. She unlocked an outer door to a cabinet that contained a suitcase sized box. She pulled the box from its secure location and laid it on the table in front of me. She handed me the key and said that it would unlock the case. She said that their instructions were to be discreet and that she would give me some privacy.

When she made her departure I quickly used the key to unlock the case. As I threw the lid open I could not believe my eyes. There were stacks upon stacks of one hundred dollar bills. I had no idea how much money it was. On top of the cash was a letter. It said, "I knew you would seek out the truth and find your way to this money. Don't worry about the rest of the family. Each has been rightfully awarded their inheritance. Hopefully this $750,000 will aid you in finding some peace." Warmth filled my body. A smile hit my face from ear to ear. I seemed to float through the bank as people thanked me for my business. I came to rest in the driver's seat of the Caddy. I hugged the case and threw it into the passenger seat. Taking a deep breath to shake off the surreal haze, I exhaled, laughed, and stated aloud, "I am truly blessed."

Without hesitation I returned to the Hotel room. I quickly pulled $50,000 dollars from the suitcase and stuffed it into a pillow case. Just then I heard a knock. It was Officer Chris. I let him in and handed him the pillow case full of money. He gave it a quick scan and said, "So what is the plan?" I asked, "Don't you want to count it?" He told me that he trusted me. I told him that we should just keep it simple. I said, "How do your guys feel about hanging out in the desert and somewhat tied for a few hours?" Chris asked, "Can you be more specific?" I told him that in order for them to seem as the innocent victims of a hijacking they had to play the part. He said that for their cut, two hours was a small price to pay. I continued telling him that as they drive through the small town of Loco Hills to stop at the rest area next to the only café. Their story is to say that one of them had to use the restroom. At that point I will appear and approach them with gun in hand playing the part of the bad guy. All they have to do at that point is follow my commands and in a few hours they will be free of the scam and richer for it. I estimate that they will be traveling through Loco Hills at around 11:30 a.m. I will loosely tie them and leave the van nearby so that they can use the radio for help. Be sure and tell them to give me as much time as possible to make my departure. Chris agreed to the plan and left.

It was now 10:00 a.m. and time was of the essence. I jumped into the Caddy and headed due east down Main Street through Artesia and drove toward Loco Hills. The road I was traveling seemed to move under my car like a treadmill as I felt stationary and timeless with my thoughts. The treadmill motioning of the road gave way to an unreal slow motion as the view of pump jacks hammering the earth for black gold drifted by. Man made work horses with no direction but up and down as they sucked the ground for oil and obstructed the landscape. There wasn't a car in site and I felt so alone. Soon the loneliness gave way to an extreme anger as I pondered my reason for the impending vengeful rage I was about to unleash. I needed to get a grip. I needed to get my head on straight. I grinned and said to myself, "I need some music." I turned on the radio and lo and behold there was a DJ with the introduction to yet another song by Clifton Dee. The DJ gave the title as "Strength." The song started out with a guitar solo that had the strength and rhythm of a vigilante heart. The lyrics that followed were as inspired as my current quest and came through the speakers as follows.

Slay the beast then have your feast.

Tomorrow's triumph lies in today's battle.
The venom deep in Satan's Rattle.

Turn your back the sly attack.
It is wisdom that you lack.

Stand firm in yourself and what's right.
Believe in that.
Watch your freedom take flight.

Peace!
Slay the beast then have your feast.

The lyrics repeated themselves one more time and the song finished off with more hard and thrashing guitar. It was exactly what I needed to hear and I no longer felt like I was in slow motion. It now felt as I was in fast forward and the landscape became a blur as the Caddy carried me to Loco Hills. I had a friend who lived here as a young teenager and had spent some time stomping these grounds with him. I remembered a semi private dirt road that led south behind the local café. I turned down that road and kicked up some dust as I spun the tires a little. After about a mile the road veered west to run alongside a ravine that would eventually give way to an opening that allowed entrance. This is where I parked my car. I grabbed my gun and started to make a hike back to the café. In no time at all I had reached the rear of the small restaurant and walked around to the front. I had concealed my weapon by stuffing it in the back of my pants and allowing my shirt to cover the handle. Looking at my watch I could see that it was 11:25 and realized that the time was near for me to finally confront my enemies face to face. I could hardly stand still. The town seemed empty as if they knew that trouble was brewing. Just as I thought that the café might even be closed a big man came out of the front door. He was clean shaven and wearing a button down pearl snap shirt. The big off white cowboy hat complemented his boots. The only thing he said as he removed the toothpick from his mouth and put one hand on my shoulder is, "Don't worry son. We never saw a thing." He turned around and went back into the café. I could see him pull the shades down as to indicate the town's approval for my arrival and their ability to accept blind justice.

I heard the thundering hooves of a horse and saw my spirit guide riding his white horse straight at me. I had not ever seen him look so fierce and ready for war. The intensity in his eyes was matched by my enraged heart and I knew that it was going to be hard not to lose my mind. I knew that the time had come and saw the corrections van come up over the western hill.

The plan was falling into place. The van pulled over next to the café and the passenger door opened. With flawless execution I pulled the revolver from my pants, pointed it at the van, and made my advancement. Without hesitation I had the gun barrel kissing the temple of the guard in the passenger seat. I said, "Put your hand cuffs on and get in the back." He put on the handcuffs and as he made his way behind the front seats I followed while still holding a gun to his head and closing the door behind me. There was an area between the front seats and the back cage that had two seats on the outside edges that faced each other. The handcuffed guard took one seat and I took the other. I told the driver to do as he was told and neither of them would get hurt. I told him to take the dirt road heading south and to follow it until I said stop. Not once did I look back at my enemies. There would be enough time to look them in the eyes when they received their punishment.

The driver ended up along the ravine where it opened up to reveal my car. I told him to stop next to the Caddy. When we came to a complete stop I told the driver to handcuff himself to the steering wheel. Still pointing the gun at the other guard, I told him to get out of the van. I followed him out and told him to go over to the rear of the Caddy. I opened the trunk and grabbed some rope from the plentiful supply that was there. I told the driver to release himself from the steering wheel, put the handcuffs back on and step out of the van. With both officers outside of the van I told them to go over to the nearby tree and sit with their backs to the tree. Now that I had them away from the ears of my enemies, I told them quietly that their involvement would soon be over. I loosely tied them to the tree with a long rope. I thanked them for their cooperation. The driver looked me in the eyes and said, "If it happened to my Grandpa, I would do the same thing." We nodded in agreement as if we were all in complete understanding of the situation. I thanked the officers again, grabbed the key ring from the driver, and returned to the van.

With my heart pounding almost out of control, I unlocked the back doors to the van. I could see the two objects of my wrath. The orange color of their clothes would soon be adorned with splashes of blood red. I could feel the immense pressure of hatred build inside me. I had to hold it together just a little longer. I unlocked the cage door and told the two shackled pieces of scum to get out of the van. They did and I then told them to both get into the trunk of the Caddy. With the realization of their impending doom, the weaker one started pleading with me and asking his partner to do something. I could not stand to hear his voice and punched him hard in the throat. The stress must have got to him as his knees buckled and he fell to the ground. I was about to explode with anger and vented a little by kicking him in the face as he fell forward. The other son of a bitch started to run. I made short work of his efforts by shooting him in the leg. Hearing sounds come from their mouths enraged me even more for I felt that they should not even exist. I grabbed some duct tape from the trunk and quickly wrapped it around both of their heads and mouths. With what seemed to be super human strength, I picked up each enemy separately and stuffed them into the trunk. At first it seemed as if they would not fit but it's amazing how cooperative broken limbs become. As I shut the trunk a clap of thunder rang out simultaneously. I could not have choreographed such a coincidental scene with sound as if the closing of the trunk couple by roaring thunder signified the doom of those inside. I walked over to the guards and asked them for one final favor. I asked them to allow me to put blind folds on them and explained to them that they never saw what I was driving. I told them that the inevitable down pour of rain would take care of the rest. I thanked them again, returned to my car, and drove further west along the ravine.

The road was a little known back road that led back to Artesia eventually. As I made the several turns and dips I could see that the rolling black clouds were here to wash away all evidence of my stop in Loco Hills. It was as if the Great Spirit saw fit to cleanse me of wrong doing and to sanctify my future actions of retribution. The rain lasted for about 10 minutes and gave way to the sunlight as quickly as it had rolled in.

I remembered a steep Cliffside that was just around the next turn and how it used to have the biggest ant bed I had ever seen. Pulling alongside the location, I stopped the car and got out. I could see the formation of the ant bed that was about 6 feet in circumference. It was very noticeable how the huge army ants gathered tiny pebbles and grains of sand as to surround the entrance that led to their underworld. I realized that the tiny insects were underground at the moment but would soon be making their appearance as the warming sun was now beating down on us.

I heard pounding coming from the trunk of the car and floods of rage began to consume my existence again. I decided to get some rope from the back seat and was glad that I came prepared with long metal stakes that I had been saving for just such an occasion. I hammered four stakes in the ground on one side of the ant bed. Each stake was located in distance from the others to accommodate a stretched out person on their back. For some reason, I thought of snow angles and how in this instance it would be dirt devils flailing about on the ground. I moved to the other side of the ant bed and hammered four stakes there as well.

Quickly I opened the trunk of the Caddy and began to remove the dumfounded idiots with great ease. I felt as if I could lift anything at this point. First I threw the bigger one over my shoulder. He made a great effort to get loose but to no avail. I slammed him down hard against the ground and could hear the wind leave his body in a resounding thump. He would not settle down so I gave him a punch to the face that left him unconscious. Without hesitation I stretched out each of his limbs and tied them to the stakes. It took little effort to put his partner in the same situation on the other side of the ant bed.

The big one was now back from being unconscious and turned his head to the side to see that his partner was in the same predicament. I now felt as if there were no limit to the amount of torture I could bestow on the two. I circled them as they looked up at me. I looked hard into their eyes as the image of them beating my Grandfather kept surfacing in my mind. I yelled down at them, "How did it feel to beat an old man?! Did you enjoy inflicting pain on my Grandfather?!" My eyes swelled with anger and my vision turned red. My spirit guide was in the distance and I heard the steady beat of a drum as he danced around as if to prepare for war. The beating sped up and I no longer felt as if I was walking around my prey but floating and advancing in sections to the beat. I remembered the long handled sledge hammer in the trunk and retrieved it. Both of the scum bags seem to realize at that moment that they were in for a long torturous event. They began to scream and whimper under the duct tape. I asked them, "Did you hear my Grandfather wince in pain?!" The question was followed by me swinging the sledge hammer as hard as I could down on one knee of the big demon.

The hammer seemed to separate his leg and sank into the hard ground beneath. I made my way around each of them and drove the long handled sledge into each limb at the joint. With every blow I would ask a question out of completely enraged sorrow for my Grandfather. Blood was now spreading on the ground and soaking my enemies. My focus was now entirely on the big one that seemed to me as the leader of the two. I pulled out a knife from my pocket and unfolded the blade. I sat on top of the evil eyed bastard and grabbed him by the hair with one hand and lifted his head. With the other hand I waved the knife in front of his face and asked him. "When you threw him down his well to die could you see him moving?" At that moment I sunk the knife into one of his eyes just enough to puncture it but not to kill him. I then asked him, "Did you say anything to him with this tongue of yours?!" I cut a slit in the duct tape. I had some convenient pliers to pull his tongue out of his mouth with one hand while the other hand made a quick slice and cut his tongue in half. The weaker partner started to scream under the duct tape and I could not help but continue my rage by jumping on top of him and pounding my fists over and over into his face. With every blow I was imagining the night they beat my Grandfather and threw him down his well leaving him there to die a slow agonizing death. My fists were completely numb and my enemies face was no longer recognizable as human. I jumped up and kicked the one eyed bastard as hard as I could repeatedly in the head. My blood was boiling so hard I did not know if I could ever regain my sanity. I began to circle around the two devils while trying hard to regain my composure. I focused on my breathing which must have been nonexistent for a while because I was now gasping for air. I leaned over, inhaled several breaths, and began to cough a little. I wiped the tears of anger from my eyes and proclaimed to the sick bastards that death would be too good for them. I said, "May you be cursed with many years of extreme pain in order to contemplate fully what you have done!" As I began to turn around I noticed the ants were making their way from the hole and started to surround the beaten demons. I smiled with great satisfaction, jumped into my Caddy, and drove away.

Chapter 12

Hope

Now that I had unleashed my own demons and cast them upon the two murderous idiots, I felt a little more at ease. I had one last stand to make and then I was unsure of what direction my life would be heading. The realization of being locked up for taking the law into my own hands began to take place of the retribution satisfaction. This Caddy had to be destroyed because it was a link to me. I remembered a scrap metal yard south of Artesia and as the back road let out onto the main highway I headed in that direction.

It was good to see that the operation was still in full bloom. A crane, giant fork lift, and a car crusher made for an excellent evidence disposal. I pulled into the parking lot of the business and walked into the office. There was a portly man wearing a white sleeveless undershirt, smoking a cigar, and laughing at the television. He was sitting behind a counter as I made my entrance. The man looked up at me and asked, "What can I do for you?" I replied, "I need that car outside to be eliminated." He smiled and said, "We get a lot of request for that." "So do we have an understanding?" I asked. He walked around the counter, put his hand on my shoulder and asked me if I had some back up wheels. I told him no but that was going to be my next question. The cigar smoking man said, "I will eliminate your car and sell you that old motorcycle outside for $5000 dollars." As I handed him some money I replied, "Here is $10,000. That should cover the hush money fee as well, agreed?" He said, "Indeed it does my good man, Indeed it does."

The cigar man said that he had to go to the main yard to get the motorcycle keys and in an effort to save us some time he would take the Caddy. I pulled my suitcase from the car and waited next to the motorcycle as cigar man drove the Caddy into the wrecking yard. He parked the car in an ideal spot for the crane operator to pick it up. As he approached a small office he pulled a hand held radio from his belt and apparently communicated with the crane operator. Cigar man entered the small office and quickly came out with some keys. He started walking back to me as the crane operator picked up the Caddy and swung it around into the smasher.

Cigar man handed me the keys and said, "Good Luck." I thanked him, strapped the suitcase on the back, and started the motorcycle. Just as I was driving away I could see the old Caddy being crushed and could not help but be a little sad. I thought of all the situations that car had seen me through. As I looked down at the motorcycle I hoped that this mode of transportation would serve me well through one more act of vengeance.

By now I was getting very hungry and realized that I had not eaten since lunch yesterday. I knew that I must give myself some nourishment. I could only think of one place that could fill the hunger I now feel, Old West Burgers. It is the burger place my Aunt Delores owns and runs. It is also the place of contact I had informed the beautiful Keisha as the place she could try and find me. I was very eager to find out if anyone had left word with my Aunt. My mouth began to water at the thought of one of her fantastic burgers. I speed up and the front wheel lifted off the ground a little.

I pulled into the parking lot of the little joint and made my dismount. I grabbed the suitcase full of money and walked into the restaurant. Aunt Delores was busy taking and filling orders for the drive through customers. Without looking up she said, "Have a seat anywhere. I'll be with you in a minute." I sat down in a back corner booth so I could see all who entered. After a few minutes Aunt Delores made her way to the dining area and said, "Oh my goodness, where the heck have you been Tristan?" I replied, "I have been to hell and back." She said that she would whip me up a feast in a jiffy and be right back. She quickly returned with a huge double cheese burger complete with fries. She had also brought a batch of her delicious steak fingers with gravy for dipping. She went to the window and turned the sign around to read closed. Returning to sit with me she asked, "Is everything ok?" I explained to her that if all went well that everything would be ok. I told her that I had one last order of business and then I probably would not ever return to Artesia. She nodded in understanding. As if she could read my mind she told me, "You know your father is a member of the old Church in Hope. They are having one of their week long revivals. My son in law's parents attends that church and tells me that your father is preaching in tonight's meeting." I quickly devoured the meal and thanked Aunt Delores. She told me that she would inform my mother that I was alive and well. We hugged each other and I could feel her shake with emotion. She contained her composure with just one tear. I assured her that everything was going to be ok. Before I left through the front door I stopped, turned around, and asked, "Has anyone left a message for me?" My Aunt said, "No. Why?" "Just checking," I replied. I exited the front door, strapped the suitcase on the bike, hopped on, and drove away.

It was now 4:00 p.m. and I was well aware of the church meeting times of 7:00 P.M. I had three hours to contemplate my next moves. I pointed the motorcycle to head west down Main Street in order to revisit the town of Hope one last time. The summer air was cleansing and brushed through my body as if to purify me for the next task. My spirit guide was loyally galloping in the distance and the motorcycle hummed with anticipation. As the landscape started to roll with signs of foothills the town of Hope appeared in the distance.

I drove through the one horse town to the other side where I could visit the gravesites of many old relatives. I parked the motorcycle along the road and began to walk toward the old graveyard. It felt as if the aged resting place was in the middle of nowhere and beckoned for attention. Hearing whispers of those who have passed away, I carefully stepped through and around burial plots. I read the head stones as I respectfully passed through. Some I recognized and some I did not. As I began to turn and head back to the entrance, I notice a head stone that stopped me dead in my tracks. The stone had an epitaph that read,

It feels so good to shed my skin and bones,
No longer one of physics drones.

Emerging now into the spirit,
Angels singing, can you hear it?

Shed no tears and do not weep,
Through heaven's gates I do now leap.

The bottom of the head stone had the born date but no death date and was etched with the name Clifton Dee. I could not believe my eyes and thought to myself that one day I shall surely have to meet this man.

Feeling truly inspired by my visit to the old resting place, I returned to my motorcycle and drove over to the Penasco River for some further reflection. I remembered swimming in an old water hole that was part of the river and hoped that it was still full of wonder and life. As I approached the remembered site, I could see a young girl. She was about 10 years old and wore a beautiful white dress that draped her completely. Her hair was as golden red as the summer sunsets and flowed in waves that ended around her waist. The pure white dress she wore revealed only her hands and bare feet. She seemed to dance in rhythm with the wind as her hair and dress followed. It was the most graceful thing I had ever seen and I wondered how real could it be. I knew that I was either seeing things or that I was in the presence of an angel. She glided over the top of the water as if she where ice skating. Just as I was about to advance toward her, a beam of light shined down from the sky and she vanished.

I thought to myself, "What in the world was that all about?" I felt as though I needed a dip in the water in order to regain my sanity. I dove straight into the deep end of the water hole. As I came out of the water and took a deep breath, I could hear my spirit guide let out a battle cry. I looked at my watch and could not believe that it was already time to right the last wrong.

I jumped on the motorcycle and with the wind and summer heat, I quickly dried. I drove back to the small town of Hope and turned into the parking area for the old church. The front doors were wide open because of the lack of air conditioning. My timing was impeccable as the congregation was ending a gospel hymn. I could hear everything that came echoing out of the front doors. I could hear the unmistakable voice of the man I once called Dad. He said, "Let's get out our bibles and turn to the gospel according to Luke." I could not stand to hear his voice and took it as my cue to enter.

As I made my way up the steps and into the church I bellowed, "How about let's turn to the truth according to Tristan!" Everyone in the church turned around to take a look at the person who dared to interrupt the service. Preacher man looked at me and said, "Tristan, good to see you." I replied, "It's a damn shame that I can't say the same." The congregation gasped at the profanity. Preacher man said, "Son, let's go outside and talk." I quickly replied with an angry voice as I grabbed the gun from the back of my pants, "I am not your son and no one is going anywhere!" I pointed the gun straight at the podium and the church people made a simultaneous inhale out of fear. I quickly told the congregation to not fear for it is not my intention to hurt anyone except the devil who is on stage. I made a quick inventory of the people and saw a young girl setting next to an old woman. The girl looked exactly like the angel I just saw down at the river. This was a good sign to me and I knew that I was on the righteous path.

Still pointing the gun at preacher man, I said, "Let's talk about a fleshly betrayal between father and daughter. I want this congregation to know of the sexual abuse you rendered to your own daughter." Preacher man said, "Son you must be mistaken." I replied, "Bullshit!" and pointed the gun at him harder as if to demand the truth. Preacher man held up his bible and shockingly enough tried to justify himself by saying, "Even in the bible, Noah lay down with his daughters." The congregation gasped in disgusted revelation. At that time I pulled the trigger and shot preacher man in the hand that held the bible. He looked as if he could not believe what I had done. He held his gunshot hand with his other. Just then a shot rang out. I felt a bullet hit me just above my right hip and make a through and through flesh wound. I turned to confront the shooter and saw a young boy about 13 who looked so frightened that he could wet himself. He had a smoking revolver in his shaking hands which he dropped on the floor. I walked over to him and said, "That's ok boy. You are just doing what you feel is right. I respect that." I picked up his gun and told the congregation that this will all be over soon. I told them that I just needed to share some thoughts.

I told the people, "You know hope is a funny thing. I hope that you people will now realize that just sweeping bad news under the rug is not the way to deal with things. My sister tried to tell us all about the wrong doings of that man up there years ago and instead of doing something about it the ignorant people of the church just looked the other way as if nothing ever happened." Just then preacher man said, "I did nothing wrong." His repeated denial infuriated me further so I shot him in his knee. The young red headed girl who resembled the angel stood up and said, "It's true! Preacher has been doing bad things to me and told me not to tell or God would punish us all." The congregation gasped in realization. I said, "You see, you people live in a blind forgiving way that is cowardice. Acting like nothing has ever happened has allowed evil to rape the innocents of your children. I have seen the fleshly demons manifest their ugly heads into a dysfunctional lifestyle that has rendered my sister incapable of many things. She will never have a healthy relationship with a man. She turns to drugs to numb the pain of betrayal. She will never have a normal life. It is all because of the twisted mind of that man you people allow to preach at you. Come on people, wake the fuck up! I hope that you will understand my situation. I hope that you all can allow me an unscathed departure. Above all I hope that you will never take the word of a child for granted."

I told the people to all get up and walk to the front of the church to the door that led down into the basement. I told them that I needed them to remain in the basement for 10 minutes as I made my departure. I could tell that the people where now in full cooperation and understanding. As they walked toward the front, I heard preacher man groan on the floor. I could not stand to hear him any longer. I walked over to him and landed a kick so hard into his crotch that I knew he would lose all ability to use his treasured tool of degradation. I took a nearby wooden chair and swung it over my head and directly down on his face. With that blow he was out.

The young boy who shot me and his father were the last two to enter the cellar. They stopped and looked at me as if they agreed with everything that transpired. The boy's father looked at me and said, "Good luck Tristan." I replied, "Make sure justice is served." He said, "Looks like you have helped that to happen." I asked, "Will you allow me 10 minutes for departure until you call the authorities?" The man smiled and said, "How about 15." "Even better," I said as I turned and walked toward the front doors.

I exited the church to a sight more beautiful than I could have ever imagined. It was Keisha. She was standing there looking at me with her loving blue eyes. Her long beautiful brown hair was riding the curly waves of the wind. She was holding the hand of her son Billy. Next to them was my new friend from Montgomery, Jason. I could not believe my eyes. I walked over to them and said, "What a sight for sore eyes. How the heck did you find me?" Keisha said, "Your Aunt said that you might be here." I looked at Jason. He said, "Man I was just traveling and got hungry. It was purely a coincidence that I chose Old West Burgers at the same time Keisha was there." I laughed, looked up at the sky, and said, "It might be more than just coincidence." I had forgotten about being shot until Keisha said, "Oh my gosh, your bleeding!" I assured her that I was OK and asked, "What are you driving?" She pointed to a black SUV. I said, "Do you mind if we all travel together? I don't think I'm in any condition to drive that motorcycle." She said, "Absolutely." I went over to the motorcycle and retrieved my suitcase. We walked over to the SUV. I said, "Maybe I should lie down in the back." Keisha, Billy, and Jason got into the front seat as I lay in the back with my suitcase. Keisha said, "Where should I go?" I looked out the window and saw my Spirit Guide look at me with a satisfied nod. He leaned back on his horse with his spear and threw it into the sky toward the south. I told Keisha, "I hear the cantina business in Mexico is pretty good." I looked at Jason and said, "Are you in?" He said, "Sounds good to me, my brother." Keisha put the vehicle in gear and we started to drive away. As we began to put a few miles behind us, I started to realize my situation. I got the girl, got the money, and got my vengeance. With happiness and relief filling my spirit, I started to laugh uncontrollably. Young Billy looked back from the front seat and asked his mother, "What is wrong with him?" Keisha and Jason looked at each other, smiled, and in unison said, "He's blessed."

About Author

Clifton Dee was born in southeastern New Mexico in 1972. He now lives in the northern Texas Panhandle. The author began to write in 2008 as a healing release. To his surprise the words came flowing into formation. "Between Hope and Nowhere resolved itself of its own volition. I feel as if I am just a conduit that channels words from something much more mystical."